SPY THRILLER

THE SLEEPER SERIES

THE GODS SMILE ON THE BASTARDS

By Anna Schlegel

BOOK THREE

Translation from Russian

Schlegel Press Association

The Gods Smile On The Bastards by Anna Schlegel
Book Three of The Sleeper Series

Published by Schlegel Press Association
Friedrichstr. 123
Berlin, Germany 10117

ISBN: 9780999127629

First Edition: April 2017

Translated by Alla Koshechkina
Cover photography /Fotolia

"...The Sleeper Series is a modern, fast-paced spin on British Intelligence operations that offers an entirely different perspective on why intelligence people become defectors."

- MSNBC

"...spy novel, promising to unravel the tangled web of a strange couple caught in the middle of an espionage game of British intelligence."

- The Huffington Post

"...a thriller that begins with a couple's discussion about intelligence processes and evolves to a cat-and-mouse game played out across the streets of Europe."

- Midwest Book Review

Also By Anna Schlegel
THE SLEEPER SERIES

MONEY CAN'T LIE
Book One of The Sleeper Series
Should there be three pieces of crap, this is of the British Intelligence classic.

WHO SPREADS FOR WHOM
Book Two of The Sleeper Series
The British intelligence cannot compromise its integrity, it will adhere to its principles like in the old times of rock 'n' roll. And it's damn good to look at it working... but then it's scary to see it work against you.

ONLY ONE REALITY THAT KILLS
Book Four of The Sleeper Series
It happens to everyone without exception. It will inevitably happen to you unless you live under the wing of the legend.

LIE MAKES ME LIVE
Book Five of The Sleeper Series
This game of the intelligence, we were either to see through it, or die.

Also By Anna Schlegel

THE DEAD BANK DIARY SERIES

THE DEAD BANK DIARY
Book One of The Dead Bank Diary Series
The rats living on the refuse of the bank's backyard stay full at all time.

FOR THOSE IN THE SHADE
Book Two of The Dead Bank Diary Series
You may live your whole life without getting to know who you are, and sometimes this is for the better.

THE PRINTS ON THE SNOWS OF YESTERYEAR
Book Three of The Dead Bank Diary Series
The best one to rob the bank is the banker himself.

SOME DAY I'LL HIT A BANK
Book Four of The Dead Bank Diary Series
The bomb lives to its internal time.

THE FROZEN DEBT
Book Five of The Dead Bank Diary Series
When totally nude have a look, maybe you still have the shoulder loops.

CONTENTS

Author's Note

The Gods Smile On The Bastards

About The Sleeper Series

Chapter One Invisible Handwriting

Chapter Two There Ain't No Fool

Chapter Three Schumann's List

Chapter Four Backup Men

Chapter Five The British Job

Chapter Six The Money Trail

Chapter Seven Sonofabitch

Chapter Eight The Living Bomb

Chapter Nine Stronger Than Life

Novels by Anna Schlegel

About the Author

THE DEAD BANK DIARY SERIES

Contact Information

AUTHOR'S NOTE

What do the defectors really want? Why do these people betray their country and friends? Why are some of those defectors lucky, while some others are not? Why don't they ever have any regrets?

What are their true motives? Is it about money? No. Do they do it for fear? No. Do they sometimes wish to build their careers in this alternative way? No. Are they seeking fame? No. Have they been brainwashed? No. Can they be naive idealists? No.

Whatever answers you may think of, all of them would be probably wrong.

Are they betrayers? Yes, they are. Are they doing the right thing? Yes, they are. Do they find in this treachery what they must have been looking for? They sometimes do. How can they live with this? They are perfectly in tune with their own selves.

What are their goals? Now you will have the answer. It is worth knowing. This answer will surely change the way you see the world. This will be the answer from the legend.

Once you are able to see the intelligence's handwriting, you may see the words of failure inscribed in the same handwriting, telling of a failure they are yet unaware of.

THE GODS SMILE ON THE BASTARDS

In looking at that other man from afar, he found it hard to shake off the feeling of observing his own self from the outside. That other man resembled him way too much. The man was better than him, more experienced, and he looked more convincing, and rather like a slime ball. Everyone could see it. The man succeeded in making everyone believe he was truly him, in person. And the man could prove it.

What could eventually happen if the man slipped away? Then the only guy remaining would be him. And he would be constrained to be more like his former self. For all those long years, he had plain forgotten what kind of a person he was, underneath. He would have to recollect and become somewhat more life-like. He would hardly be able to make it, really, unless he was dead. But then, would that be a preferable option; something they truly wanted?

Why do intelligence people become defectors? There may be two answers. One is obvious. They become defectors due to a landmark case against some other turncoat. Every agent, while keeping a close watch on the case, usually dissected the defendant's mistakes so he thought he would never do anything similar, convinced that he could be smarter, employing a lot more caution...

The second answer is something else. People come to be turncoats long before they start working for the spy directorate. So, read it all: this is worth knowing. This is the answer from a legend. Listen to it, give it a touch, and you'll be blessed with the smile of God.

ABOUT THE SLEEPER SERIES

Each of the secret services has its own handwriting, faint and hardly perceptible. This handwriting is their custom, it does not change for years and one can read it through. This handwriting can lead the agent to failure. This is what these books are written about, if anything.

These books also tell of the legend that keeps recruiting people across time and distance, of something that is stronger than life. This legend is an eternal truth, refilled with the living blood of every new recruiter that would choose the way of the legend. These books are on the legend Kim Philby.

These books contain neither facts of Kim Philby's life nor any historical events. This is all about the modern-day and pure fiction.

I'm giving an answer to the question: Why the legend of Philby would be everlasting? Why is this legend of Philby of such a deadly pulling power? How do the people survive under the wing of his legend?

There is little said about it yet this is the main point.

They become traitors long before they step across the threshold of the spy directorate. They step across expressly to turn into traitors one fine day. That is the way they see their career. They wish to re-act that life of the icon. The legend of Kim Philby is making them traitors from the moment they open that book of his or read about him. This legend keeps recruiting people without money or contracts. The reality is forceless against it. The legend keeps dictating its own logic. It may come along imperceptibly, once the book of the legend is read through and half-forgotten, it would sprout up deep inside and live to its own time, so one day it would casually remind of its existence, in an implicit way, and push its follower to take the decision to which he must have been prepared since long, with just an occasion being in short supply.

Most paradoxically, such agents appear to be more mature, like everyone who does not really care much about public recognition, awards, money, appreciation and all those matters in connection with a regular rewarding career, they do not really fall for the uniform and regalia. Surely, the traitors gain incomparably better money, but it was not always this way, and would never be the main point. These people rate themselves so high that money does not measure that value. They are essentially free.

For such people there is no borderline where they become traitors, they must have since long slipped across by taking no notice. These people are usually well-educated and highbrow, and as much intelligently cruel and deeply calculating.

They are idealists. The philosophy of theirs makes blood turn to ice. This is how the legend of Kim Philby works. And that's a damn good British job.

CHAPTER ONE

INVISIBLE HANDWRITING

Berlin, February 2011

How long had we stayed there with Vlad, already? It must have been a month or so. It seemed like an eternity due to our fear and anticipation of the unknown, or because of this empty, frost-bound house in the suburbs of Berlin where the snow scratched the windows with a gentle clink. We had been hidden behind its walls as if we were cut off from the world – the world of espionage. The careers of so many people were being thrown up in the air, the investigations were underway, and they kept searching for... Oh my god, could they have been searching for the Russian group that dissolved twenty years ago? But for what reason? Had not they managed to find Vlad until now? No way. Vlad could have been since long arrested or under surveillance, and this would have been impossible to mix up with anything else. There was nothing like that. So, there must have been something else. There must have been something of more recent vintage; something fresh, like this icy wind that kept biting my face and which carried from some place afar the faint odour of freshly baked bread and the smell of gasoline.

Vlad said, through his teeth, *How long can we keep sitting in here? My balls ache and are swollen,* and he got to his feet and in one motion drank a pownie of vodka in a single gulp, then screwed up his face and went to the loo.

"Should we get a porn magazine?" I cracked a joke when he came back to the kitchen.

"There is a mirror down there. I still take a liking to myself." Vlad waved the comment aside, whether in fun or in earnest.

Vlad kept saying what he had on his mind and whatever came into his mind without much mincing words, as if he really wanted to tell me everything, the sooner the better, so that I'd start thinking the way he did so I could finally be able to take his place in the scheme from which he'd been incidentally knocked out from by the British Intelligence.

Or did he really believe that he could set his own brain on me? True, this was exactly what he wanted, and maybe there was more to it. I failed to understand right away what I was about to get from him. Vlad was so free-spoken. I realized his storytelling could be rather delicate and scarcely perceptible, kind of like the smoky taste in whiskey. I had no reason to catch him out, and I was telling lies myself every single minute, so they were nothing much. Surely, at times, he would hold something back; but I noticed that as time passed, he would still tell me. And I'd been thinking so until recently, until a few days later, when in doubt … and no, I had never really cross-checked him. However, either time or necessity took its toll and I finally got used to thinking just like Vlad, during the days I'd stayed with him. It was unavoidable, since I had no information. I was clueless and just wanted to make sense of what I was supposed to do if I was to replace Vlad. I had no wish to be his backup in precisely this way. It was frightful to think that I could remain, while Vlad would be there no more.

He was no longer Vlad Holt, but I continued calling him Vlad and nothing more. He still remained Andreas Leman, a common businessman. But could it last for long?

Vlad feared losing this surname of Leman more than anything; it had become his true name for the twenty years he'd been living in Berlin. He had a sick mother. He never spoke about it. He probably had a woman...or a man... shit, he must have fucked half of Berlin. He was a bright, high-bred blond with silver temples and a pale face, with a sharp bird-like nose and dry, delicate frost-chapped skin, so his freckles were hardly visible, his eyebrows and eyelashes seemed whitish, as if covered in snow dust, and his eyes looked pale, frozen, and transparent. One of his eyelids, somewhat lopsided, concealed his ever-tolerant look.

Shit, I never knew those kind of men existed in real life; I had only seen his kind in the old photographs of the Third Reich. He had the sensuous charm of killing power; and not because it revealed a young shaver, but because he was a genuine bastard. When looking at him, I kept thinking that to properly love him, one also had to hate him so very much. That is why men loved him, as women, for the most part, love in a different way. He possessed a hell lot of confidence; the kind an expensive whore has, because she knows she can do whatever she wants. And he kept doing it. He kept getting rid of the partners and middlemen in the business, who could put it at risk, choosing the means without much thought and chopping them away as if he had a knife and could cast them all aside with no regrets.

He was pressed for time, to preserve whatever was left of the scheme. And every single minute he risked becoming yet another dead witness for the court. So how could he keep on with this feeling for all these days? How could he keep smoking quietly and eating the mini cakes out there? He must have been thinking it was over, all this time, taking notes and reviewing things.

So what? Did he really think that he would be able to read through the handwriting of the British Intelligence?!

Well, he was sure the handwriting of the secret services never changed, so it was quite legible. It was probably the only thing that remained unchanged for many years. The rest, including the game rules, the game itself, and the toys that the secret services usually played – all of it had changed. Yet, the hand was still the same. As for everything else, Vlad was rather helpless. What could he possibly do? He was a sleeper agent, Harvey Smith, who had been incidentally burned up as a witness for the court when action was required. He had never been an operative, neither at this point nor twenty years ago. He was a financial expert; a damn good one.

He was not thinking of escape. I'd been begging him to flee. He could have dissolved with no trace, just like salt. But he had no wish to do so. What was this self-destructive stubborn streak? So he remained there, glued to his laptop all day long, reviewing the press articles he had purchased on several disks to avoid an internet connection. We used to pick up cell phones when we were downtown. Every evening before falling sleep, through the half-open door I could see him hunched over the desk in his white T-shirt, his pale face and narrow spectacles lit with white screen light. When waking up in the middle of the night, I could still observe him sitting there. The darkness seemed to devour his silhouette and leave a white, ghostlike gleam that floated through the cigarette smoke.

How was he at all able to figure out what was going on, if we could see nothing and no one there? Everything seemed to be the delirious creation of his brain. We kept drinking vodka, making a snack of those mini cakes.

In impotent rage over this total nonsense, I asked him, *So why do you keep searching to identify that fucking handwriting?!*

"The handwriting will lead the agent to failure," Vlad responded calmly.

Handwriting is the kind of habit that eventually kills. One cannot just break off a habit; it appears rather powerful, something like heroin as the system for which the agent works, is bigger, stronger, and more heavy-footed than him, making everyone conditional on its long-term targets. And people get used to it, so they do not really notice; as if it were an illusory reality that remains unnoticed unless it fractures like glass. Eventually, it kills its agents on its own.

But how could one see through this invisible handwriting?

Time passed, and we kind of got used to the thought that there was no way out for us. It was also impossible to for us to keep hiding here for long. The house had fallen into disrepair: the dim light leaked through the dusty windows and the rooms were sprinkled with this light as if they held ashes. The long and empty corridor was filled with brick rubble, so when stepping out the door, I seemed to walk out into a winter garden, the black soil of which was covered with rotten red apples. It was cold in there, and somewhat bare-bones, with a similar smell to that of wet soil liberated from the melted snow and recent punk.

Yet, something made me take a detached view of Vlad. I had the feeling that someone else had appeared by his side in an imperceptible and delicate way, as though it were someone's light breathing. I started thinking in my own way, and destroyed our intimate world. It broke up accidentally, in an absurd way, as if a cup had slipped out of my hands and flew into fine splinters. It seemed that way to me, initially. From all those things, Vlad had told me there was only one thing I had to understand: that there was no possibility of coincidence. He'd said that the reality in this game could turn out to be a mere illusion of mine. However, the illusion could also turn out to be a wall against which I was like a dry autumn leaf – and not just me alone. There were many others; so many, and they'd been there before me and would surely come after me. This illusion was stronger than life, and it could sustain itself by recruiting people across time and space. I would have never thought that colliding with it could be so painful to me; it was as if I'd been taken by the throat with someone's hands.

CHAPTER TWO

THERE AIN'T NO FOOL

Early the next morning, I walked out to the pay phone and heard a hurried, agitated voice. It was one of the partners in the deal speaking. He said that he was nervous and requested an appointment with Vlad later in the day, at the railway station.

It was quite understandable. The deal had been put on freeze for an indefinite term. The partners were somewhat more cautious after we'd lost the bank.

It was a high risk for Vlad to go out. After hanging up the phone, I caught myself with the thought, *Hang it all, I'm in Berlin! This is Berlin!* and I dropped in at the hairdresser's. And I went out as a blonde with a bob, with fair eyebrows so that the freckles on my face turned to be even more visible. I paid a visit to a secondhand shop, where I found a women's coat similar to that of Vlad's. It was nothing special: straight and formal, a dark gray in color. Upon returning to our house, without taking off the coat, I put on Vlad's hat the way he used to wear it, low down over my eyebrows, and then, after twisting in my hands his round matte-mirrored sunglasses that he used to put on when he went outdoors, I put them on too, and looked at myself in the mirror with an indistinct look that concealed my face.

Vlad's reflection blinked behind me in the mirror.

"Karl just called. He wanted to have a look at you, just to see you, so that he feels better," I said, and smiled at his astonished face. "I'm in Berlin! Why haven't I guessed earlier? I'll draw less attention like that."

"Yes, you'd better go; it should calm him down. You are looking damn good; just like me in the best of times."

At the railway station, Karl noticed me from afar. I passed by him under his troubled look and, by barely meeting his eyes, imperceptibly gave him a nod, then quickly walked away. In the evening when I went out to use the pay phone again, I did not hear any message from him, so he must have relaxed a bit.

Meanwhile, the legal action seemed to pick up steam. The prosecution had a witness, Harvey Smith. This meant that the man would be able to prove in court that he was the true Smith, a sleeper agent. He would prove he was the real Vlad. He would actually prove he was a far better witness than Vlad himself. And he would do it in a quite professional manner, as there seemed to be no other way, since they'd already had a dead witness using the same name. But how could he manage it all? God only knew. Apparently, he would somehow manage to do it; otherwise he would not have turned up. And where could this son of a bitch have come from?

At that time, we had no idea that Vlad was no longer Harvey Smith.

The previous witness had taken the name of Vlad Holt from Vlad. As Vlad said that if someone took the name of Andreas Leman from him, he would be hardly able to make it through life.

It was incredible. The banker Martin Schumann was accused of money laundering. Besides him, the money laundering case involved Deutsche Bank, Dresdner Bank, and Kommerzbank. Schumann's only fault was that his bank appeared to be the smallest bank. It was not so difficult to obtain, from that kind of bank, any information on transfers processed through the other banks by a certain Russian company who was the seller of military equipment. That company appeared to be an easy target for a scandal. The banker Schumann found himself under pressure. He'd turned out to be somewhat more resilient than expected, so the American side was ready to nail him on espionage charges for the benefit of the Russians. What a weird accusation it was, wasn't it? Schumann had left the United States twenty years ago. For this kind of an indictment, there should have been proper, valid evidence.

Some old defector could have recollected that Schumann was recruited by the Russians twenty years earlier, during his internship with a minor audit firm. But it looked like the man had recollected something of higher significance. The defector in question had already died of heart attack.

Vlad decided he could make another dead witness in this legal action against Schumann. What else could he think, having worked in the same company with Schumann when he lived under the name of Harvey Smith and being recruited about the same time? Schumann had been given away and covered for by the MI6, but even more ridiculous, this Schumann must have been the source the British intended to conceal by all means. For that reason, there'd been too many figureheads that resembled the source.

It was clear Schumann had found a witness for himself on his own accord. It was Smith; someone Vlad had been playing a while ago. Vlad understood he could make a dead witness. Vlad was mistaken. The British Service had already procured a dead witness with the name of Vlad Holt, codename Smith. As the man had turned up twice as a dead body, it was clear they must have started to investigate Schumann long ago, and the man was not a harmless sleeper agent.

There must have been something major in connection with Schumann; something worth the effort of the intelligence guys. One way or another, the charges of espionage looked doubtful. It was not hard to disintegrate – it seemed to have started moldering away like sand – but then something else happened, in Langley. It looked like an explosion of an old bomb: quiet and invisible to everyone around, followed by major check-ups, dismissals, and the launch of a series of investigations. As ill luck would have it, the "bomb" was in connection with the Russian group that used to work in San Francisco and New York, where Smith used to be. It was so deadly careless of Schumann to have found a witness that pulled him into this spy scandal, which appeared an even deeper downfall compared to what it had been. It became clear that Schumann would hardly be able to walk out of court just like that.

The Russian group that dissolved twenty years ago was made of agents that were either auditors or the owners of minor IT companies. Those companies were used as channels to buy up Russian foreign debt; the bills that had ended up being privately owned. Where could they be? Could they just like Vlad keep on living a plain unremarkable life, long forgotten and imperceptible when left unattended?

"Vlad, what should we expect from that witness?" I asked him. "In order to come before the court as a living Smith, he should possess some fucking valid evidence. You've been telling me that you would hardly be able to prove that you used to be Smith. And what kind of evidence of being Smith could this witness have?"

Vlad didn't know what to think. If the British Intelligence had started to cover Schumann three years ago, they might well have prepared a living witness by this time. But was it really workable? How could they possibly lead astray all those experts that were supposed to monitor his every move? It seemed self-destructively inconsiderate. What kind of evidence might this witness have, of being that particular agent Smith? It could be some candid cam filming of the man next to the tomb of Smith's parents. However, this would sound rather like child's babble from the sandbox.

The witness was supposed to have some evidence for the reliable identification of himself as Smith. What kind of evidence could it be? It was normally all about fingerprints. But if there had been fingerprints, there would have never been a dead witness, Vlad Holt, or the suspect, Andreas Leman.

"That's funny," Vlad said. "I have never taken any secret documents, never placed them in a bag, and never hidden the bag under a stone in the park, let alone left my fingerprints on that very bag. I'm no fool. There ain't no fools like that. And how do they catch them, otherwise?"

Vlad said that the FBI never found such evidence satisfactory for legal action. That is why there appeared to be so many obviously-doctored frame-ups with the hideout under a stone in the park or inside a waste bin, and the capture of coded messages, including agents' emails to their Moscow spymaster. All of it created a semblance of the spy network activity; nothing else. How could one possibly use one and the same hiding place twice? Why was this hiding place next to the agent's house? How could the agent leave his fingerprints on the envelope containing the classified paperwork that he'd put into a hideout? When reading about a captured agent, it always remained unclear as to who was the fool in the story. The agent who may have forgotten to wipe out his emails to Moscow? Or the FBI staff, unable to catch the fool over twenty years? Or otherwise, the rest of the public: whoever was ready to believe this bullshit?

Vlad only repeated what he had said before. The agents were rarely caught over rubbish like a luxury car in their garage or a handful of diamonds in their pocket, or a suspicious money transfer or an appointment with an embassy employee under the bridge in a park, or even with a pen drive full of classified documentation. This was far too cheap cloak-and-dagger fiction.

Understandably, fingerprints were out of the question. They could have learned of a recruited agent only from the hearsay of some defector or a traitor who was yet another agent. And the evidence was usually manufactured some time later. But quite often, it was not even manufactured. The much-needed evidence was usually brought by an insider from the Russian Services.

So what? Could someone have provided the paperwork straight from Moscow? And wasn't the risk a bit too high for a case that was over twenty years old?

"Vlad, there was no internet twenty years ago. What was the usual means of communication for any paperwork?"

Vlad told me that documents used to be brought to the liaison agent for him to hand them over to, say, a legal counsel; and then from the lawyer's office it could be collected by some other liaison. Both liaison people were deep-cover agents and professional intelligence officers. They were not familiar with each other, and there were hardly ever any traitors among these people.

"What about the lawyer?" I wondered.

"He would immediately give a sign for the documents to be collected. No one would ever leave his fingerprints on the paperwork. There ain't no fools," Vlad added again.

"Vlad, why haven't they discovered you as Harvey Smith before now? They must have long known you were Smith." I was totally clueless.

"They must have found me. But after signing my confession statement, I'm no longer good for this legal action; and aside from the courtroom, no one really wants any Smith. I know nothing, and this is obvious. And that other witness also has no information. He would only tell them whatever they wish to hear from him. He must have been long since prepared to do so. All by myself, as Smith, I'm not really wanted; and in court anyone could pose for Smith. As you can see, this American, Vlad Holt, turned out to be a far better Smith, as he had a wife who, I guess, was an agent herself. In the same way, this witness would make a more rewarding Smith than me. There is always someone better than you. They say so, but I've never thought there could be someone who would pose as me! For my own real self! For me as a living person! Not the ashes from the urn with my dental X-ray printout, and not a frozen corpse... Can you believe it?" Vlad asked me, growing sulky.

If only we had known that time that this someone was not simply going to pose as Vlad, but would actually make a lot better Vlad than the original — that is to say, incomparably better; so as to make this live witness far more convincing than a dead one! What kind of person could he have been, for that matter?!

Vlad was hardly able to prove that he had been himself, as Harvey Smith.

Apart from some other reasons why Vlad was still alive, there appeared to be one more major cause. Not so long ago, a Russian defector had resurfaced in Boston. His name was Jan Chernov. He'd taken a look at the photo of Vlad, as that of Leman, and Jan had confirmed that this person was not Smith. Could they have believed Jan? Oh, yes. Jan had an undeniable advantage of being a living witness, unlike so many others.

Or could that witness have some other evidence conjured out of thin air? What other person could this Jan possibly identify as being Smith? Jan had started looking for Smith on his own accord. But he had only hit on the trap: a manager named Vlad Holt that used to live in New York without knowing the FBI suspected him of being Smith. Jan was supposed to remember some features, to identify Smith. Or maybe not quite his facial features, but something else? Jan could easily do without any fingerprints. What could it be, then? The simplest answer was obvious: Smith should have known something. And Jan must have realized the man in front of him was not Smith, after having a talk with Holt. This meant that Jan could have confused Smith with someone else, but he could not be wrong in what this Smith was about to tell him as agent Smith.

And would this kind of evidence be admitted in court? Just words? That was rather doubtful.

"It would be admitted if they have the name of that person," Vlad said, still thinking it over.

"Which person do you mean? That of the resident spy?" I wondered, with no clear idea of what I was asking, but recollecting some spy series.

"No, it's not so hard to find out the resident's name. That must be the name of the person who used to mastermind the group activity from Moscow. There used to be a designated unit in charge of the money; – someone to provide for the station in different countries and for the communist parties – and there also used to be someone in charge of the foreign debt buyup through a network of companies. It must have been the fourteenth department of the KGB. By the way, the person in charge also had a code name. No outsider could get to know it."

"Then... this witness... Where does he come from? Could he have been furnished by the Russians?"

"Who the hell knows? If that witness starts talking of past events; of something twenty years old, that would mean he's not been involved since then, and must be a similar sleeper agent, just like me. Any of the parties could have supplied such an agent."

"I'm not getting a thing in here, Vlad. You've been in control of the business. And this appears to have been an open secret at this point. And any minute now, I fear they might get hold of you right here due to this particular business."

"No-no. This business of ours is not a big enough piece of cake for them, as you may think. Baby, haven't you ever seen real big money?" Vlad inquired, somewhat defrosted. "I'll show you one day. We'll take a walk... once we are out of here. If we ever manage to escape. And for the time being, would you mind another mini cake?"

"I have not yet bored you to death?"

"You've got an advantage. You are not my woman, so you should make use of it. I wish to make..."

"Make your own self out of me. I've got it." I finished the phrase for him, instantly realizing that he could, damn it, really achieve this one fine day, and I would not even notice myself at the point where I turned into him.

So what kind of person would I be? And wasn't this the true reason why I was here? True – however, upon my entry into this house, I had no idea the back-up for Vlad meant an express duplicate; a cast of his. What would remain of my own self, then?

"Exactly. So could you make it so I don't worry about you when you leave? In a word: at the moment, everyone's got to extinguish the fire following the so-called "explosion". What could have happened there? I'll be damned if I know matters of twenty years ago! Could they have excavated Jimmy Hoffa right on the lawn in front of the Russian Embassy building? I don't know what to think, really." Vlad shrugged in annoyance and started smoking.

"But what is this bomb? Why is this Schumann so important?"

"They started protecting Schumann three years ago. The British must have never thought of this bomb explosion. Otherwise, Smith, the man in connection with this bomb, would not have come up as a witness. As to Schumann, there must have been something fairly recent in connection with him – some kind of operation not older than three years ago. What might he have got his foot into?"

"And then, what happened to Schumann must have more to do with the British lady, while this bomb explosion has taken place on the American side... What could be the possible links?" I could see no link whatsoever, and I looked at Vlad, eager to read the answer on his face; but I could see nothing there.

"There are no links. It must have been an incidental piece of crap," Vlad echoed.

Vlad thought they must have started to cover up for Schumann just because some particular operation or event Schumann had stepped into appeared worth this subterfuge. It must have been something of high significance. In the meantime, they must have found a convenient witness for Schumann; someone named Smith; the man who used to work alongside him for the same company once upon a time, recruited and forgotten over twenty years ago. If that Smith turned up in court as a dead man, he would have made a perfect witness. Smith was supposed to turn up in court one way or another. And he'd made his appearance twice. First, Vlad as Leman had drawn up a confession statement about him being the agent Smith. And the second time, Smith had come up in the urn with my husband's ashes; those of Holt, an office manager from New York. For the third time, Smith had resurfaced as Holt in a freezer on the bank of the East River, where he must have stayed for three years. What judge would understand?

So at this particular point, a living witness came forth, and he called himself Harvey Smith.

On the American side, Schumann was just the head of a minor bank, from whom they could get anything they wanted without much effort. But then, could these charges of money laundering have been just a pretext for them to obtain something of a higher value from Schumann? But what could it be? We had no clue.

"If they had truly wanted to accuse Schumann of money laundering, they would have done it already. Why would they speak of the espionage charges? This is weird." I did not know what to think.

Indeed, after all that had already happened, the charges of espionage seemed suspiciously weird. I kept discussing the matter with Vlad, in order to get a clue, but we seemed to be turning over the sand with heavy hands.

We were totally lost. How could we possibly learn things – and from where? How could we get information as to what may have really happened in Langley today due to the group of Russian agents dissolved twenty years ago, of which Vlad had been a member under the name of Smith? As per Vlad, there must have been no one left alive in that group. And Vlad himself had no wish to return from the other world. Why the hell? So that he could find out something that had no name?

Vlad was thinking out loud with me,

"They must have got something regarding Schumann. Or, most probably, they have someone who must have told them something about him. But the man cannot act as a witness…"

"…since the man is probably dead," I finished his phrase. "It must have been that same defector who was found dead in the suburbs of New York. You thought that Schumann must have been warned of his pending arrest, so after he realized this defector was supposed to be a witness against him, he must have killed the man. Or it might have been not him, but… This death of his has been so handy, coming right at the point when accusations were being formed."

"That is why the Americans must be searching for someone able to reconfirm the words of that defector, regarding Schumann. It must be something like that. The British side must have chosen the wrong person to provide for the coverup; this Smith. Smith would make his speech on the part of the prosecution and actually screw them up. Indeed, he could say that Schumann had been recruited. That's a fact. But then, what's more, Schumann had been put on hold. Who would ever need a sleeper agent?"

"...but it's actually Smith who's now linked to that old bomb that just exploded on the Americans," I concluded. "And the Americans must have linked those otherwise-unrelated events, meanwhile getting trapped by their own logic. Looking for links where there are none – well, that figures. They can't really sort the crap into parts. And what was that bomb they linked Smith to? Could it have been something like the Mitrokhin archives?" I inquired, with no clear idea of what I was asking him. The name of that spy scandal just happened to be familiar.

"No idea... by the way... have a look at this classic! Did you know that the second volume of the Mitrokhin archives was issued after his death?"

"So what?"

"The British Intelligence is really fond of memoirs. Some of them get published after the death of their author, and sometimes the suicide story is weird. Or otherwise, it gets written during their lifetime, with the author unaware of having written it. These are all dead ends. Do you remember my telling you?" Vlad wanted to continue, but then cut himself off by giving a wave of his hand. "The bottom line is: they are free to write anything they want in the postmortem memoirs."

"Well, the Russian Intelligence is the same kind of bullshit."

"The Russians are not in time to take their hands off, so they leave fingerprints, in which one can easily see "the hand of Moscow". The British Services usually do things with someone else's hands. They never try to convince anyone of anything - quite on the opposite – and that is why it's not so easy to find out where the British lady has been involved. But this is not the point. Something else must have happened."

I asked Vlad whether he was keeping something back from me.

Vlad responded that it did not really matter, and just snorted tiredly, "Mein herz, whether I tell you or not... It'll only make me concerned about you. Or I'll have to kill you. In what way can you help me?"

"I could break your legs so that, like in the Misery, you keep sitting here, drinking vodka together with me instead of running around, and that could eventually save your life."

CHAPTER THREE

SCHUMANN'S LIST

Vlad was supposed to give me the list of all partners in our business and then withdraw from business. But in actual fact, the list of the business participants meant pretty much nothing. It was all about people who made a difference. Would they start taking the money from some other hands? They were all humans. They were all on the market. This was a matter of price, especially in that kind of arrangement. Who would ever need that business? Well, somebody wanted it, and this undisclosed invader must have already invested millions into this takeover. As Vlad had once told me, *Should this money fall onto us in a banking package, it could flatten us as completely as a board of concrete.*

It was so easy to lose everything at once.

"Have you got any backup?" I had questioned him that time.

"Yes."

"What does it look like?" I'd wondered.

Now I knew how it looked. I could just take a look in the mirror. I was the backup. I had to become Vlada Holt, the new key to the deal; his duplicate.

Nothing seemed to have changed. I still had the same sharp face and a keen hungry look, but Vlada Holt seemed to have sprouted inside me and stuck to me as a wet glove, to become my second skin and my way of thinking. My mode of behaving was now somewhat different: I was calm and confident, and a bit loutish. This was in my blood. What could I do? I was, in essence, Vlad Holt. Never mind my female face. I had the taste and passion for the come-on game, and this essence of mine was coming out by bringing me back to my own self.

Would we ever manage to preserve that business? It had already attracted attention. And how long ago could it have happened? Would the British continue looking for Smith after they put out the fire?

In fact, the British had taken pains to turn office manager Vlad Holt into the image of agent Harvey Smith. There had been nothing like that with Andreas Leman. It seemed as if he had not been seen until his case file apparition in the Americans' hands. But could the British have prepared someone else for the role of agent Smith using the code name Andreas Leman? Or, could the British have found the true Smith long ago? Vlad and I were pretty sure that Jan had identified his true Smith. But had he killed him? We could not tell this.

At nighttime I walked out to use the pay phone. The partners in the business used to contact Vlad by leaving him a message via the voice mail of his Canadian company. Every day we waited for a call from Victor. Victor was determined to pull Vlad out of this shithouse, and by using his own contacts, he tried to find out what had really happened. Victor had been to New York and returned to Moscow, then gone back to New York, and communication with him was cut off at times and then restored again.

The whole business was made using Victor's personal links which he had later on passed on to Vlad. For Victor, he loss of the business would amount to losing a significant part of his life; but Vlad used to be a friend of Victor's and Vlad was of higher value to him than the scheme itself. I had so much reassurance, every time, when I heard Victor's voice!

The answer machine transmitted the voice of Maximilian Richter, a legal counsel and an old friend of Vlad. It was not so difficult for Richter to find out what had been underway with the attorneys in charge of Schumann's defense. He only uttered a few words: *He's bought some old personal data files out from Moscow,* before he was cut off.

Clueless, walking at a brisk pace and hiding my face from the burning wind, I made my way back to our house and, with the door hardly open, I asked,

"Vlad, he's bought out the personal data files. Who? Schumann? What does it all mean? Can you get the point?"

"Yeah! Oh, shit, I got it. The reason behind this legal action against Schumann is something totally different. Fuck all," Vlad cussed out in surprise, frozen to the spot in the middle of the room.

Schumann had bought out from Moscow the personal data files of the officers with German Ministry for State Security; those of the retirees. But what did it matter? A spy would remain a spy. When a personal data file is withdrawn from the archive records, it usually means the man gets free from his past and whatever links he might have with the spy directorate. This costs a pretty good amount of money. But, hang it all, this was still possible. Why would he have started buying out these files? It must have been ten years ago.

"Could it have been so easy to buy out the personal data files of the agents? Just come in like that, with a stack of cash, and buy them?"

"Twenty years ago, it was possible to buy the Kremlin, along with the president. Yes, the word is that the Germans used to buy out, from Moscow, the personal data files of their own officers. Why would Moscow need it? These must have been the Stasi files. They would be just gathering dust in the archives, otherwise," Vlad responded, distrusting what he had heard from others.

If this was really so, Schumann must have been buying out these personal data files at a price. Some of the agents must have agreed to be recruited and do the job for some other secret service, and some might have been entrusted with a one-time task. There must have been a reasonable cost, for them to get rid of their pasts. And for this reason, MI6 must have started to cover up for Schumann; they must have hired the agents that would leave no trace.

"And why do they intend to bring charges of espionage against Schumann, then? He's been inactive for twenty years, and he is a mere banker now," I inquired.

"Or maybe the British were not ready to share this information with the American side. The Americans might have learned, on their own, that Schuman bought out the agents. The Americans may be interested in making sure such personal data files have really landed in the hands of Schumann. So this legal action might be a good pretext to have a look at these kinds of data files."

What could Schumann have done to these files? Could he have destroyed them? Most probably; yet he must have retained the people with all that, and they probably contacted him on their own. An important point was that, even with these kinds of goods on hands, such as highly skilled and experienced agents with no paperwork,

Schumann suddenly appeared to be of great interest to all. Such agents were, indeed, a piece of gold.

Indeed, they must all have been formally out of service but, in fact, this did not really change anything. They still remained the same kind of valid source, just like their recent coworkers. And of particular interest there were the people who had formerly worked with the USA. There was a word that the retirees who'd gone abroad were, sooner or later, constrained to cooperate with the secret services. The most valuable asset of any retired agent is his memory, as the man is usually familiar with other agents, and keeps in mind some operations, of which the echo resonates for a while.

It turned out that this witness, an agent of sorts, must have agreed to play the role of Smith for the trial in exchange for Schumann's having bought out and destroyed his own personal data file. Thus, we would never really come to know who this person might have been.

Would it be a personal data file, really? Otherwise, could this witness just name some people they wanted, as Vlad suggested? It did not really matter much. It must have been a one-time task, for which they must have provided the witness with an extra facial resemblance to the old photo of Smith by means of plastic surgery. He could have been just about anyone. It was impossible to link him to any particular spy directorate. Would they ever examine him thoroughly? They would, as he was supposed to play the part of the prosecution. Would he be able to withstand the scrutiny? We had no wish to think about it. There had been no trace left of Smith, in San Francisco. The company he used to work for, along with Schumann, had long since gone bankrupt.

Where could this witness have lived for the last twenty years? He must have been able to leave the country after the disintegration of the Soviet Union; but where did he go to? Moscow? Why not? Where would this data file turn up, after the court proceedings? It would probably come up in the judicial archive records, but the judicial archives were not the kind of records the next mole could worm into.

"However, they may do without much scrutiny with that witness, since he must have told them everything they'd expected to hear," Vlad suggested, lighting his cigarette; and then he brushed this idea away. "No, they would rather examine him. They'll turn his trunks inside out and peep into his asshole. You cannot really expose an agent in court and rely on them having no wish to examine him after hearing what he says. The agent must be ready to withstand any checkups. And where could they possibly fetch him from? No one but me can be that kind of witness. Could they have really found son of a bitch better than me? I can't believe it."

"And what would he say? How would he put up the fire after the explosion?" I wondered, taking a puff right after him.

"No idea. He'll probably furnish what is expected of this kind of a witness."

"What?"

"It could be names of some other agents, or of the defectors. This is usually the most valuable information a retired agent may give; something of high value. So he must have supplied a few names already."

"How could this person have agreed to be a witness? He would have to undertake polygraph testing or whatever they have..." I was still clueless.

"He'll withstand everything, if he's not a dog's dick, and then ... In his shoes, I would have disappeared." Vlad was still thinking it over, and then he stopped, pulled his glasses up on his forehead, and startled, gazing through the window unseeingly. "They'll kill him. There is no other way. This is classic. This is how it works."

"Oh my... And could he not figure it out?"

"He must have guessed. The agents often take the job, well aware that they may get killed...." Vlad froze to the spot again, without lighting his cigarette. "Hmm, no; not this time. He is not quite an agent... If he is now acting for me, I'm no agent. Hmm, he is about to cover up for the banker, so he must be a moneyman himself..."

"Couldn't he buy the jury, along with the judge?" This silly speculation flashed through my mind from something I seemed to be reading on Vlad's face.

"True, he'll probably buy them; otherwise, what a goddamn banker he is, isn't he? I'd be disappointed in him."

As usual, two or three blocks away from the house, I inserted the sim card into the cell phone. I saw a message from Ilya. He was waiting for me in Switzerland, in the country house he had rented for us last year. I arrived back quickly, so I said goodbye to Vlad and rushed to the station.

CHAPTER FOUR

BACKUP MEN

I recollected the house as if we had been there with Ilya just yesterday, but instantly, all of it disappeared. The things that had occurred to me over this month seemed to have crossed out my whole life, now in tatters. I didn't have so much invested in it – just a few weekends with Ilya – and I'd seemed to need nothing more. But this was not really so. Ilya had a different life: he had that bank of his, his debts, creditors, lawsuits and lawyers, and finally, he had the money that attracts more money. I had nothing at all. Ilya earned his money with ease, without ever thinking about it. He just stretched out his hand to take whatever was close by, without looking, and damned was the man who, at that particular moment, incidentally turned out to be in the way. As to me, every cent did not come cheap to me: it was as though I had to chuck it out of the frozen earth with a poll-pick, like potatoes.

Ilya was pulling me in to death because I was uncertain of the road to get to him. If, one day, Ilya called me to say, *We aren't going to date any longer. I've met another woman*, it would be over. I would not be able to get him back; I had no idea how to do it. I had to change my whole life so that these Sunday evenings and nights with Ilya could continue. My gut had been telling me that if I did not change myself and leave things as they were, I would lose Ilya. Or was I just thinking this way now, at the point when nothing could be brought back?

Last summer, over here, Ilya and I had walked out to smoke together on the porch, which was slippery with dew. The blazing sun had shone in my face with the clouds up in the sky, the heavens open to their depths, and the mountains close in and standing nearby, within arm's reach. The supernatural beauty of the place was breathtaking. The air was different, heady, and held the taste of snow and watermelon.

Everything looked the same, but I saw Victor's massive, swelling figure on the porch. He smoked by leaning his elbow on the banister. He was there alone. Ilya must have been busy. If something had happened, I would have noticed that. It was only now that I came to understand why all those partners sought to have a look at Vlad in person, even from afar or for a split second, by passing in the crowd in a supermarket or in the park. Some of these people used to work for the secret services, and others were just over-cautious. It was enough just to cast a look at Vlad, to make sure everything was fine.

Several years ago, Hurst Bank had been on the verge of merger. The Russian Intelligence had been behind it, so all the partners had turned somewhat more watchful. Even so, Hurst Bank, which was in charge of the major settlement, was now lost. And if Vlad was lost... Vlad was of a higher value than the bank. How could I have missed out on that, earlier? Vlad guaranteed that all the matters were settled. Vlad could transmit this confidence with a single glance, as if putting it into your hand; and it seemed that if he had to go to the pit of hell, he would do it in a similar, even-minded way, and everyone else would follow him there. Sometimes I had a feeling that a single hand gesture of his was enough to take everyone along with him.

Surely, I would not be able to replace him. One had to be him in order to do that. My mind turned back to the witness. Would the man indeed manage to be the same as Vlad? It was unlikely. Knowing Vlad, I could say for sure that it was impossible. This was my line of thinking that time, anyway.

From a distance, Victor's face seemed dark with bristle on his cheeks and chin. He was turning gray, but his eyebrows remained black. He had pale eyes lined in dark circles, and his eyes looked transparent; his glance loutish and stony. He smelled of cheap cigarettes and of either rain or the melting snow. I could sense this smell from afar on his coat. It was the smell of Moscow.

"Victor, have you been to Moscow?" I inquired under his prying eyes.

"Yes. Ilya's failed to come. Damn it." Victor, lighting another cigarette, passed a glance across my face from under the palm that covered half of his face. "There is something else I wanted to ask you: whether you sleep over with Vlad. I now see that you don't. It would be absurd for him to fuck his own self."

"Sometimes he looks at me as if I were a spouse he has no chance to divorce." I smiled at Victor and thought that things were a lot easier with him, compared to Vlad.

What had been on Vlad's mind? Once, I'd caught sight of a minor list of names among his notes; something as in his other listings. And I'd asked him, jokingly,

"The short list: is that of the people you had no time to sleep over with?"

"Yes. This list is for you," Vlad responded. "Is it okay that we don't sleep over?"

Vlad was no different from other males. They usually viewed me as an object they could purchase. Indeed, Vlad rather liked me, but he looked at me as if I were a thing he would rather sell. What could I do? He was a moneyman and a son of a bitch. From that look of his, I could see that my price was rather high, and I thought, *You're a profiteer, cupcake.*

"I don't give a curse for your ass," I snapped, still unaware of where this conversation was heading.

"Really? You can't take your eyes off it," Vlad noted.

"Couldn't we do without harlotry?"

Oh my god; I had since long forgotten my job as a trader, when I used to change men like panties. Apparently

Vlad hadn't heard this, so he must have been thinking of something else,

"I want you to remember this list."

The first line contained, like many other lists of his, the name of Maximilian Richter.

"Isn't Richter a friend?" I'd asked in surprise.

"He's a friend. Did you think that I only get rid of the enemies? There can be neither friends nor enemies. This is business, so things are different. Richter is an element at risk. I wish I could have him within easy reach, close at hand. I mean, your hand reaching at his balls. Is that clear?"

"You... oh my god... You're a monster."

He'd made me speechless.

"You're the same. Do you think I would be wasting my time on you, if you were any different?"

He was right. One day, Vlad had told me that I perceived him as being like a cannibal at the missionary. I used to look at so many men the same way. True, I liked him, this damn good-looking man. But time passed, and I was either used to him or started seeing something else in him – or perhaps I feared seeing something painfully similar. Why hadn't I seen it earlier? Everything could have been different.

"And in what way have you been losing time with me?"

"I sometimes look at your butt. You've got none at all. Very beautiful. This definitely costs me half an hour, daily."

"Oh my goodness, what shit."

"Do you mind having a smoke with me, bunny?" Victor asked.

I took a seat by his side on the porch,

"Have you managed to find out anything?"

"It's a load of shit. You'll tell Vlad everything."

It was Victor who had decided I should be a backup for Vlad. But when did he make this decision? I did not want to think about it; that must have been long ago. Victor had since long arranged for my ID documents in the name of Vlada Holt. I had no idea if he had been thinking that I was able to act as a backup, or if it had been accidental, and I was an option of last resort. It did not really matter. Victor was always somewhere far away, but I knew that in case a failing bank or some scheme of sorts turned up, he would still call me, just like now.

Victor had not been able to find out everything, but he learned quite a few things about the witness who'd turned up in court under the name of Harvey Smith.

The man was advanced in years and used to live in New York and San Francisco. For the last ten years, he'd been in Moscow. How could they have convinced him to do this job? Who could tell? Could it have been for money? Had he been a part of the Russian group, along with Vlad? This was something we had no knowledge of.

"In what way could he prove that he is truly Smith?" I wondered.

Victor said that, for this witness, the legal action was probably a task he was getting paid for. Could he have been recruited by any of the parties? He was hardly of any interest to them. Otherwise, his case file would not have turned up at all.

"A case file? From nowhere?" I asked, perplexed, lighting my cigarette from Victor's. "How is that possible? Can they just walk in, in Moscow, and grab the agent's case file from the archive records?"

Victor had no information; everything he had was mere speculation.

However, one thing was clear: this case file must have turned up just recently. But then, could the witness have come up lately, also? Oh my god, just imagine… the witness steps in from nowhere, very much to the point, along with his own case file. Fuck-up.

Victor knew that Schumann had become a middleman at the exchange of an American agent against an ex-Stasi officer, who was doing his term for espionage in the United States. And he said that Schumann would not stop there. There was a word that the man was ready for a second exchange. But no one seemed to know anything for sure.

But where could this case file have come from? And whether it was a true case file or not, we did not really know.

But even with it being so, the task of carrying the case file from the Moscow archives could have been performed by either a madman or a double agent, who must have taken the file subject to approval from his management. But why would anyone carry the file out, if it was good enough to take pictures of the same? Bullshit.

Victor said that the first thing that came to his mind was: there must have been a fat mole in Moscow who worked for the British. The British should have thought a hundred times before presenting this case file in court, because to present this kind of file before the jury meant to expose their fat mole and give him away to the dogs. One could count on one's fingers the number of employees with access to the archive records. It was easy to identify such a person. If that was true, the mole must have been arrested by now. They might have lingered with his arrest until they had a good reason to do so, and now they must have found a trigger. Why would the British have decided to unveil their mole just like that? Could it have been a double agent that brought them misleading information? Whatever the case, it was hard to conceal that kind of mole. He must have been identified long ago, and the British must have known this for a while; yet continued to play cat and mouse.

However, it still felt wrong. If they had found another mole in Moscow, there would have been some scrutiny and hearsay. There had been no word on it. The case file itself appeared of no interest now, twenty years later.   The file from the Stasi had been given away easily because it was outdated. But Moscow never did things that way. This kind of a case file from Moscow could only have been carried out by a mole.

"And it doesn't smell of a mole," Victor said in contemplation.

Or had this Schumann bought the file out? But then, where had this forged file come from?

Surely this case file was a high quality forgery – however, be that as it may, the case file must have been fabricated with the consent of Moscow, as the witness was clearly a Russian agent. It didn't matter whether he was either a sleeper or an operative, but he had been indeed recruited twenty years ago by the Russians when he lived in the USA. He was able to disclose the recruiting technology of those years and of the banker Schumann having been recruited; but then, after moving to Berlin, the connection must have been cut off.

In a word, the story appeared to be the murky ravings of a madman. Could anyone confirm that this was a genuine case file? That remained unknown. Everything depended on what the witness could tell and on his behavior when in court. The man was expected to be rather convincing. And even if he was the true Smith, he would have to make a damn good effort.

To Victor, it was clear that Schumann would not be able to walk out of court just like that, if he had something to do with that "bomb". What could be possibly done there? Victor also thought that the witness would flee after giving his testimony. And then the whole legal action would turn into an epic farce. With a dead witness and a runaway, both of them named Smith, it would be way too much.

"How can the judge withstand the whole story?" I mumbled, lighting another cigarette.

"He could not really stand it. There will be a different judge," Victor replied in a quiet echo.

"And what about that Russian group? Have you managed to find out anything? Or did the witness say anything about it?" I asked.

Victor managed to learn about a few people from that Russian group. They'd been all arrested at different times, and none of them had been nailed on espionage charges. There was no evidence. Three of them had been arrested five years ago. They must have been under FBI surveillance. Why hadn't they collected any evidence?

"There was no evidence," Victor said, as if he knew this for sure.

"Then what was there?"

"Nothing but the intention to make them into spies."

All three men had been accused of money laundering. What had been their activity, as agents? To whom did report? One of them had been caught after his appointment with a Russian diplomatic official. Could a Russian briefcase have really been meeting a recruited agent? For what reason? Just for a chat?

"It can't be that the group has been working, and there is no evidence," I said, bewildered.

"It can be. They must have been backup men."

"Backup men? What does that mean?"

"They are not the guys from that Russian group. They are Russians living in the USA. They must have imitated the agents in a rather convincing way; enough to arouse suspicion while furnishing no valid evidence."

Each of the secret services had those kind of agents. They were normally recruited on site among non-professionals, then received some training, were paid, and received assignments that could be performed by a qualified agent. And from the speed at which they were being detected, one could assess the professional competence of the FBI counterintelligence. Otherwise, they could be designated cover agents, well aware that sooner or later they would be identified. They were expected to play their agent's role in the most convincing way.

"Victor, why have you called me out through Ilya? What's it all about? What has happened? Have you learnt something regarding Vlad?" I finally asked him, clearly understanding that this appointment was probably something more than mere precaution.

In Moscow, Victor came to find out that the group had been given away by its spymaster. But, had this been really so? The word was that he had been leaking information for years, even while being really cautious, and that is why there had been no arrests. They sometimes kept an eye on the deep cover agents for many years.

"Then Harvey Smith would have been known to the FBI," I suggested.

"The spymaster must not have given away all of them. Why? Can it be so? No way. It can't be true." Victor shrugged, lighting a cigarette and pressing its crimpled filter with his canine tooth. "I admit that there could be the case files, a death certificate, and even a grave..."

"A grave?"

"Yes, if needed. The spies normally have unmarked graves, bunny. This is damned Moscow. There ain't no rules; but for a traitor not to give away every one he knows – that can't happen. The spymaster is doing his term in a Moscow prison, now, charged with espionage. I'd like to have a look at him."

There was yet another story. As it turned out, the spymaster was an CIA informant – not directly; but surely through some intermediary, with his information reaching the CIA. So the decision had been made to discreetly carry him to Moscow. Upon the receipt of a special request from Moscow, they must have called the spymaster, Smith, and two other people from the same group. The latter must have been informed that the spymaster had been invited to face trial in Moscow. Yet, this invitation for the spymaster must have been, in fact, just an excuse for them to carry Smith to Moscow. There was word that Smith had been an CIA informant. They'd given him this assignment, to accompany the spymaster, so that the man could not smell a rat and escape.

"So what? Did they arrive in Moscow?"

"Yes."

"But then, Vlad should have also been in prison."

"Exactly. I don't know."

"Oh my god, is Vlad considered a traitor? I can't believe it."

"It happens way more often than you'd think," Victor spoke in the same calm manner, without taking the cigarette from his mouth.

"And what do you think? Is that okay?!"

"Vlad will remain a friend of mine until he proves the contrary, by himself. I can't believe anyone anymore."

CHAPTER FIVE

THE BRITISH JOB

"By the way, Jan will also act as a witness. He would recognize Smith. Someone has to do it, anyway," Victor said.

During my last appointment with Victor in the airport, he had made a passing reference to Jan. This time, Victor recollected his encounter with Jan in no hurry, as Jan now found himself in Vlad's place. How many people were to be interchanging reflections of each other in the mirrors of this legal action against the banker, for a legal action that had not yet started?

Jan was lucky to be discovered after they'd found Vlad. Jan would have no fear for his own life, as the judge would not have accepted yet another dead witness.

During those years, the British had given Jan away to the Russians. He was of no value for them; they must have milked him dry. Jan had intended to escape and go live in the UK, but he had left for Poland by happenstance, only to find out that he had been exposed. It had not occurred to him that the MI6 must have given him away after depleting him. He was burnt up by the people for whom he'd been working for two years, who had promised to carry him out of the country. This was life. Who would ever need him? He was someone to be paid, to be provided assistance in employment, someone to take care of and nurse, and someone who would cost them money. Jan had been unable to understand it for a while and kept thinking that he had been betrayed by someone inside. It must be said that the man had been driven to think so. There was no going back. So Jan found himself in the US Embassy. They'd carried him to Boston and extracted whatever he still had in store, then issued him a green card and plain forgotten about him. Jan was left to his own devices.

However, unlike Vlad, he was not a sleeper agent, and turned out to be mere rubbish. Jan found it hard to put up with this; and who wouldn't? He wanted to find the person who'd betrayed him.

Who might have told him it was Smith, the man who used to live under the name of Vlad Holt in New York, who had the comfortable life of an office manager with a wife and three children? The Russians? Heaven knows. To say the least, upon giving this Jan a tip regarding Holt, the Russian Intelligence could have at one fling at resolving two different issues. Jan would have tipped off the FBI about Holt being Russian agent Smith, in the meantime, by sidetracking Vlad's suspicions, and they must have already been thinking of getting rid of Holt; so if Jan had chosen to kill him, this would have been quite handy.

Jan must have started searching for Smith – not right away, but a few years later, and one day he came to Holt's house in New York. He'd intended to kill the man, but something must have stopped him. After having a talk with Holt, he must have understood that this was a different Smith, and this particular person had nothing to do with the intelligence.

Had Jan continued his search? Could he have found the real Smith? And then, if he had, whom could he have found? Who could have turned out to be his true Smith?

"Victor, could it be that the witness in question is indeed that very Smith that Jan had been looking for?" I suggested.

"Why not?" Victor had no clue.

Victor, as distinct from Vlad, was able to do more than guesswork only; he could actually find out things. What on earth could Vlad do, being trapped with me in that empty house? Victor did not draw any conclusions and intended to find out everything down to the smallest detail. For this matter, he had to go back to Moscow once again.

Had the Bureau, one way or other, found out that Jan had seen Smith in person? What was the source of this story of Smith betraying Jan, and Jan looking to kill him? The spouse of the defunct Vlad Holt might have known this. Could she have recognized Jan as the man who had once come to their house in order to kill her husband, as Smith, three years ago? Who could have killed Vlad Holt? Had it been murder, really? As per Jan, he had not killed Holt, and he appeared rather trustworthy.

Could the British side have kept a lid on Jan by holding him back as another available option in case things went wrong?

The pathways intertwined in a rather surprising and weird way. Jan had searched for the man who had once betrayed him with the intention of killing him, and he would have probably killed him. But for the time being, he was supposed to act as the British source and stand by the British, who had earlier disposed of him as of a dead load. In fact, in those former years, Jan had worked for the British. Would he work for them again? He would – he had no choice. Jan must have understood the situation; all the more so because his life was at stake. By naming the witness as Smith, Jan averted suspicion, since his intention might have been to kill Vlad Holt as he was taken for being Smith. For Jan, this appeared to be a paying proposition. According to Victor, if Jan was no fool, he would identify the agent Smith as this new witness.

"Victor, tell me: isn't it weird that Jan, after he realized the man in front of him was not the real Smith, had no wish to find the true Smith?" I asked.

"That's the point. Jan is not the kind of person to calm down. He would have continued looking for Smith."

"Given that Jan was shown a photo of Andreas Leman who was identified as being Smith, and he told them this was not Smith, does that sound like mere precaution? Or could Jan be so determined that he'd made it all this way through and eventually found the "true Smith"? And that man turned out not to be Andreas Leman. But who? Could he have found someone else – someone he might have considered to be the "true Smith"? What if Jan had killed the man?... Some kind of Smith turned up in court. Is that the man that Jan considers to be the "true Smith", whom he didn't have a chance to kill, yet? Oh my god, it looks like such a mess."

"Yet another Smith? No, it can't be so. Hmm... let us toss out Vlad Holt, who's long dead. Now, we may have a Smith, whom Jan probably considers to be the "true Smith". And there is another Smith; the one who turns up in court. Can it be one and the same Smith? Or are there two different Smiths? Fuck if I know," Victor cussed out, lighting another cigarette.

"How many Smiths are there? Vlad was thinking to fuck him up. But then, he'd be fucked making it with every one of them. There are more of them than all those duplicates of Elvis Presley."

"Could this defunct Holt have looked like a remarkable fraud, so they provided yet another Smith who was better than the original? Then the question is, for what reason? Was it to cover for Schumann? It seems highly doubtful. I guess this witness must have come up from somewhere on his own. Schumann would have been just fine with a witness like the spouse of the defunct Holt. Or was it, indeed, a real good British job?"

"Well, and for how long would they make us enjoy all this classics? Vlad must be tired to death of this classic, already!"

Victor said that after his conversation with Jan, it entered his mind that Jan was no longer looking for Smith. He seemed to have started looking out for Smith to convince himself what he had known all along. He must have understood that the MI6 had given him away, but he probably found it hard to believe. The point is: when an agent falls under suspicion or is given away by another agent, they start cross-checking him. It's not so hard to notice this kind of crosscheck. It's more like the quiet rustling of leaves, from which one may tell that someone is getting close. There can be petty requests like carrying some envelope with paperwork or refilling personal data, or maybe meeting with someone. If the agent is given away by alien secret services, for which he used to work earlier, his treachery is obvious; so there are no checkups to follow.

Jan had never been checked. He must have, luckily, been out of Moscow at that particular time.

Victor said that whatever might have happened twenty years ago, Vlad would remain a friend of his. Traitors never change. They are not given a chance to change. At first they betray the people they know or could have known, and then they become witnesses in court and give testimony against the people they don't know. That was the usual practice.

If Vlad had been a traitor, the deal would have long since landed in the invader's hands and the invader would have been informed of each and every partner and middleman in the business, and he would have gained something over many of them. But nothing like that had happened.

"Vlad is not that kind of person," I said; and for me it looked obvious.

"Yeah, they milk the traitors dry and cast them out. Vlad would not let them do the same to him. He's oversensitive. And he values himself rather highly. It's not in his character."

"Shall I tell everything to Vlad?"

"All and everything. He knows more about it than anyone else. Let him think on where this shit may come from."

While waiting for me, Vlad bought some mini cakes and consumed almost all of them. I did not know how to tell him all this. I had no clue what to think, had I? Vlad had been in Moscow?! Why had not he told me earlier? Because... it could not be true.

The things I told to Vlad appeared rather shocking, to him. After barely hearing me out, he said,

"I need to be by myself for a while."

Two hours passed, and I could hear Vlad in the kitchen making coffee. Then, through the half-open door to the smoky kitchen, he called me in.

"Vlad, have you been unaware?"

"I don't understand how it could have happened, and who else could have known I'm a traitor?"

We exchanged glances involuntarily, and I hastened to shift my glance.

"I guess everyone around have known, except for me," Vlad concluded.

CHAPTER SIX

THE MONEY TRAIL

We were smoking and drinking coffee. Vlad seemed somewhat lost; he kept eating his mini cake. Looking at him absently fiddle with the cake with his spoon, I thought that he was about to chase away the bitter taste.

"Vlad, have they been calling you in to Moscow?" I inquired warily, putting aside his saucer with the mini cake.

"Yes," Vlad nodded.

"And?"

Oh my goodness; if he had never mentioned it earlier, I would have not understood a thing. This month full of conversations had not passed in vain, as I was beginning to understand certain things that otherwise would not have entered my mind.

"I didn't go to Moscow. I stole the money from the company and left for Johannesburg. I was really scared, and scurried away," Vlad looked aside.

"What?!" I was struck dumb for a moment. "Vlad, why haven't you told me it was you who'd stolen the money? You've told me the money theft used to be some kind of frame-up; that they kind of paid you with that stolen money in order to get you recruited. From your words, I understood that they must have blackmailed you with the fact that you'd allegedly stolen your company's money. So this was not true, was it? It's actually nothing out of the ordinary. I can understand that it must have been no big issue for you to steal the money. But why didn't you tell me? I used to be a trader; I am able to understand all those things. I could actually understand it better than anyone else. You what – have you been thinking to click with me?!" I meant it a joke; yet I could not smile.

"Actually, you only understand the money talk. This is what I thought from the beginning. And I was not sure whether you could understand that no one ever paid me anything. I've just recently realized that you would be able to understand. Why should I know this? The money and blackmail are a good enough way to recruit people; this is clear. I would have told you, if I were talking to you now and not a month earlier. I didn't want you to see me as an idiot that lives under illusions."

Yeah, damn it, it flashed through my mind, *twenty years ago they must have been still been recruiting the idealists, despite the fact it was all about money by that time*. Vlad did not want to show it; but this was a fact. He only just now was telling me about it. The money must have been of no interest to him. Holy shit – he was a real moneyman, and... And so what? What happened when the illusions crumbled? It was rather weird. Vlad did not really look like a disappointed cynic, as if his illusion – well, if it had truly been an illusion – protected him like invisible armor.

"Vlad, uh... you...Was it not about the money, then?"

"Is it so insensible? A genuine illusion will persist even when you stop believing in it," Vlad remarked with hardly perceptible annoyance. "I've got nothing at all.

And if you are thinking of the deal, I won't really steal from my own pocket..."

"Sure enough. No-no, it would never come to my mind to think that. Was Victor aware of it?"

"You see, you still ask that question. That is why I haven't told you this from the very beginning. No, Victor is unaware of it."

"Vlad... is there anything else?"

Vlad said that during those years, a call from Moscow usually meant that the person in question was considered to be a traitor, and this meant the end of everything: an interrogation followed by a trial and a term in prison. And many people, when going to Moscow on call, realized it meant a term in prison for them or, otherwise, a fusillade; and that there was no way back. The same had happened to his spymaster, who was still doing his term in prison.

Indeed, I'd been thinking about this, and whatever Vlad might have done there was all the same to me. I seemed to have learned about him enough to understand one simple thing: whatever he might have done, it meant there must have been no other way out. It meant that anyone in his shoes would have done the same thing. If

Vlad had killed someone, any other man in his place would have killed, too. Everything was fine with him.

Upon receipt of that call to Moscow, Vlad had not known what to think was in store for him and his spymaster. Had his spymaster been under suspicion? Vlad used to have a good understanding of things that his spymaster was capable of doing, and what he could not have done. He could not have been a traitor. He was a pure idealist and a long-standing spy who had worked as a deep cover agent for a very long time; for fifteen years.

The point was about Vlad. Vlad had received a proposal from the British Intelligence via Richter. He was supposed to tell this to his spymaster. But his spymaster had received a call from Moscow by that time. So if Vlad had told him, he would have had no chance at all. With nothing left but fear, he had made the decision to flee.

Now things started to fit together. I had, earlier, asked Vlad jokingly, *Don't you think the British lady is taking care of you?* Vlad had replied that this was possible. For some goddamn reason, they must have wanted Vlad alive. Or could it be something different? Could he be still alive just because they might later need him, as in the sudden death of the agent Smith? Vlad was sensitive as a wild animal; he could not have missed out on this possibility. This must have been why he had not escaped. But he was totally right to think that there was no escape from the British Service. The point in question was: why did they need him? It was obvious that Vlad still had no clue about this.

"Vlad, twenty years ago… What happened?"

"I have no idea. There must have been some fact that was considered reliable, over these last twenty years. Then this fact must have suddenly turned out to be a well-made forgery. It might not have been a fact, as such, but some kind of information. But what could that have been?"

There might have been several possibilities; but none seemed big enough to backfire today. Supposing there might have been a traitor in the group. What could he have known? He must have known what was going on in the companies involved in the buy up of the old Russian foreign debt. It was no big deal for an auditor to draw these conclusions. He could have communicated, for instance, that Russia had refused to restructure the African debts under the Paris Club terms. Otherwise, these debts would have been considered war debts; in particular, the financing of the Russian ideology in Africa. In that case, a country like Angola would be free to not repay their debt. This information was worth considerable money. If that were not the case, he might have been able to reconfirm that Russia would continue to service their foreign debt despite the default. This information probably cost them millions.

Vlad lit a cigarette and then, after a couple of whiffs, told me,

"This is all fucking awesome; but it's not the point. It's over and done with. I guess the matter is not the Russian group, as such. Could the point in question be the pathways though which the KGB money was going? The money trail is the people. But what could I possibly know?"

"You are the one person who might know things."

"Do you think that someone may need the channel through which the KGB used to carry out the money and, perhaps, might keep doing so?" Vlad took a draw at his cigarette, expelled smoke, and then said, "No. This is not so difficult to see. Money of all kinds leaves a trace. The trace of the sizable public funds is as obvious as the sunrise over your head. There is no problem detecting it, is there?"

"Vlad, fifteen years ago they hired Kroll to uncover the "party funds" and they haven't found any."

"Haven't they? Are you kidding? Haven't they found it? I had no idea. Did they have no bookkeeper?"

Vlad said that the money was carried out through a network of foreign dummy companies; yet it was usually clear who was doing the job, whether it was a single wealthy person or a well-organized group. The difference was so visible. Only the blind could have seen none. I did not quite understand him, and asked a silly question: "Can you so easily tell by which channel the government money flows away? Can you see the money trail, or the path of the ex-KGB?"

"As damn clear as I can see you now," Vlad snorted.

Vlad shrugged his shoulders. This was not an issue, to him. He said that it was not so difficult to see just by reading the press reports. In fact, it'd been a long time since he'd read any newspapers for that purpose; but once it caught his eyes, he absorbed the news of a private company's attempt to put a lien on a Russian fighter aircraft at the air show, and one on some Russian property in Europe. It seemed ridiculous. Russia would never give away their property to anyone; they would only give it to themselves. They arrested their property using someone else's hands. No matter that these greedy hands could belong to a minor private company. Then a Russian oligarch could buy up the controlling block of the bank which had provided loans to the same private company. That was it: the circle was closed. It was, indeed, a well-tuned channel for carrying the money out of the country. A whole team must have worked on it; people in charge of serious government funds. It was the money trail of the ex-KGB. One could enjoy observing it by just reading press articles. It was not so difficult to see. It was an arrangement of stunning beauty.

"Fuck me gently... Vlad, that means that the point is not the money, and not that you may actually know the ways by which the secret services take the money away..."

"Exactly. The money was the first thing to come to my mind. However, if the people that we are dealing with are no fools, there must be some other kind of crap. And why the fuck would they need me? Or does it only seem to me so that they still want me? Or then, maybe, they still might want me as a dead man? That must be the simplest explanation."

I did not know what to say, and stumbled. Vlad asked me,

"Shit, do you really think I'm an FBI informant? Still sitting here? If that were the case, there would have been no ashes of Vlad Holt; neither the freezer with that corpse of his, nor this unknown witness in court who calls himself Smith; and I'm sure the man would be able to prove this is actually Smith. It's the way the British usually work, but not the FBI. If I were the Bureau informant, I would already be testifying against Schumann – no matter that I never knew the man."

Vlad fell silent, and then, looking into my eyes, he asked me, "Mein herz, do you feel uneasy with me?"

"No, I've been through this with Victor. His wife died. It was due to him. That time, Victor had asked me, *What if you'd known of Ilya having killed someone... would it have made any difference to you?* I replied that it did not really make any difference. I was in love with Ilya, whatever he was; be that a cemetery watchman or a maniac. To me, it did not really matter what he could do... I realized that it was the same with Victor. It did not matter much to me what kind of person Victor was, and what he was about to do. I did not really have many people close and dear to me. Victor was dear to me. Vlad, whatever I might learn about you, whoever you turn out to be, and whatever you do... it would not really change my attitude towards you. So it makes no difference. Just think of what kind of shit it may be. Keep thinking. You've got to make your way out of this."

I did not know, at that time, that I was mistaken.

There was nothing for it but to wait for what this witness had to say.

In fact, this Smith appeared to have solid protection, with those two backup doubles. It meant he was worth all the coverage and was more than just a plain agent.

We only guess's that after they'd started the cover up operation for Schumann. Upon finding the most suitable witness Smith, the British must have discovered that Smith had been already backed up by Vlad Holt, an office clerk with three children. The embassy translator, Michael Brown, had told them of having recently seen Smith in Berlin under the name of Vlad Holt. The British must have been ready to offer the court Mr. Holt's ashes, having staged it as a sudden death along with a source of theirs, the man's wife. However, Jan had said that he'd seen Holt three years ago in New York, and that the man was not Smith. After this, the body of manager Vlad Holt had been found in a freezer.

There was also Leman. Leman lived his life in no hiding. There was nothing special about him. The British might have intended to bring to court the dead body of

Andreas Leman, as that of Smith, but Jan had not identified agent Smith as being Andreas Leman, either. And, taking a detached view of the above events, upon discovery of Holt's body in a freezer, they must have started to consider Leman as yet another fake; a kind of Holt.

Who could have been agent Smith? As a point of fact, it could have been just about anyone.

There was yet another question: might the British be aware of Vlad's acting as Smith? The proposal of recruiting may have come to the surface after a while, and once it was there, it seemed as if they preferred to forget about Vlad. But could it have been in connection with the recruiting? Hardly so.

For the British, it must have been more important to find out why the sleeper agent Smith had been provided such a deep cover. Vlad believed he could survive until they found out.

It appeared easier to kill Jan. Jan was, in fact, the only living witness who'd seen Smith and who was able to identify him. But then, from god knows where, living agent Smith stepped in, in person. So Jan must have turned out to be rather handy. Jan would not refuse to recognize Smith as that new witness.

"Is it that the way, really, Vlad? Would Jan recognize the witness as being Smith? Bitchin' — it's become such a mess."

"True, he'll recognize him, so this witness could extinguish the fire of that old bomb. You should understand me, now. You're not a mere duplicate..."

"They must have said the same to the others, didn't they?" I cut him short in annoyance.

"I haven't finished: you'll find it worse than the others, since you are me."

"Uh-huh — just a dick is missing."

"Sometimes you don't really need one."

"You should know better," I snapped.

CHAPTER SEVEN

SONOFABITCH

At nightfall, I went out to use the pay phone, and after dialing the number, I heard Richter's voice,

"Get to the station café tomorrow at eight o'clock in the morning."

What could have happened, if Richter could no longer wait for Victor to give him a call? Had the investigating judge submitted the case to court?

Vlad was not sleeping yet. He was making noiseless circles around the kitchen by taking a seat with a cup of coffee and then getting on his feet again to lit a cigarette with indifference, then tossed it side to take another stroll from the doors to the window, followed by another cigarette that he also left untouched. What could it have been;

something that Richter preferred not to trust to voice mail? In the morning Vlad, after waking me up, eventually went to have some sleep.

Berlin, Train station

It was heavy snow, wet and gray, and the city turned dark with its humid facades and the glass of the skyscrapers that had no reflection and exposed the black insides of the sleepy morning offices. Had I come out too early? The city was still in its sleep and there was not a bit color; not a single sound, as if the minutes of eternity had passed, cold and sticking to my face and fingers, along with that snow. Closer to the railway station, where the crowd got thicker, it joined in and dissolved in the gray light inside, mixed up with the bright lights of advertising.

I noticed Richter from afar: he was sitting in the corner with a cup of coffee, his coat was open, and he had a white shirt and a white face... I had a feeling of having seen this face and its crumpled whiteness a hundred times before. I was probably looking at him as if trying to recollect what I could have had, but still did not have. This kind of man appealed to me. He was advanced in years. He had an overripe and world-weary face, with rigid and frozen traits. I could see he was free from any limits; there was not a hint of the lie line that we usually cross, well aware of crossing it though we know there is a way to forgiveness, as well as a path back. For him, everything looked plain as a field, with truth and lies. He had lies in his blood; it was part of his independence, and it was in such a plenty I seemed to be able to bathe in it like sea water.

He had that particular clear and deep look to his gray eyes, and, looking at his hands, I unwillingly thought that I would find it a pleasure to die there under his gaze.

With the words, *Do you mind?* I took a seat beside him.

Richter slanted his eyes at me and started back a bit, snapping through his teeth, *Do you mean it?* He gave me a sign to keep silent and started telling me things.

Before court, the witness seemed ready to talk about almost everything. It could not have been otherwise, as he was supposed to act as a witness on the part of the prosecution. They talked to him for a very long time. There'd been two sessions with the lawyers; one of which Richter attended for a short while, and the rest he'd heard about from the other lawyers in-between the usual tattles.

According to Smith, he'd lived in San Francisco for twenty years under the name of Harvey Smith, and he used to be a member of a Russian group that consisted of recruited agents just like himself and some deep cover agents.

Richter said that this witness Smith, *Let me call him that, for the sake of simplicity,* Richter said, screwing his lips a bit in a smile, was shown both the photos of Leman and Holt. He'd failed to conceal his recognition of Leman. According to Smith, he'd taken Leman's passport due to its resemblance to him, but then later on he'd come across the man, just by chance. Leman must have understood that Smith was living under his name, and Smith had right away decided to change his name to Holt. He'd suspected that Leman had learned of him living under the name of Holt. He'd thought that this Leman was a sort of petty drug dealer probably interested in hiding his true identity under someone else's name. Smith had also mentioned that it must have been him who hinted to the man about how to assume someone else's name. At that point, it had been rather handy for Smith. Leman had purchased an apartment in the name of Holt, unaware that he was providing the cover for the latter.

As per Smith's words, Holt had been living in New York unaware that two duplicates of his had turned up in Berlin. But this was nothing but his word. Supposing he had been living under the name of Leman, and then under the name of Holt – who would ever be able to prove it? And was it actually worth doing? Taken altogether, it was all about a twenty-year-old case of identity theft. No one would remember it after the court proceedings. While Vlad had purchased an apartment in the name of Holt and his neighbors could identify him, this particular witness appeared to have nothing but words.

This Smith had stepped in with his own Russian passport in the simplest name of Ivan Ivanov, which was as good as John Doe. The main thing the man had told them was about Leman being a mere businessman - Leman, who'd unwillingly covered for him. He had not recognized Holt in the photo. He'd said that upon his departure, someone must have seen him in Berlin. This seemed to involve high risks and they had probably provided him protection after his departure by giving a tipoff to the FBI that he'd left for New York under the name of Vlad Holt. He really had no idea as to how they might have arranged for this coverage.

Smith seemed to be telling the story and recollecting things as if he had, indeed, been living all those years in San Francisco while working as an auditor. He knew the names of parents and neighbors, the names of the streets and cafes, remembered the blackberry pancakes, his college, and the professorial chairs thereof. With each and every turn, he'd named his teacher and the dog of his...

"Holy crap," Maximilian quietly cussed out, "...you should have seen their faces as he gave the name of the dog! Some of them instantly jumped on their feet and left; some for the loo and some for coffee."

The man kept telling his story as if he'd been there yesterday. How could he be so convincing? What was it? Could it have been hypnosis? What could the Russians have done to him? Had it been a brain transplant? It shouldn't have happened at all. There was no time to train anyone so well; not in a year, not in ten years. How would he know so many details? With all that being said, the man was an auditor, that motherfucker: plain and unpretentious – a genuine one, one hundred percent, as if he had just walked out the door of the accounting office. He was apparently an agent recruited by the Russians, that sonofabitch.

He'd told them everything they must have wanted to hear and he'd told them what only a Russian agent could have known, by naming the unit in charge and the names and the code name of his supervisor. He'd told them that after Berlin, he'd been living in Moscow for a long time, and this was obvious, as he'd somewhat forgotten the language. He'd been examined by lawyers, psychologists, analysts, and a whole fucking team of experts, per Richter. Smith had been rather self-composed. He had neither faltered nor winked, and he'd responded to every question without much thought. Several times he'd consulted to his lawyer, and two or three questions had been disallowed. He had given no reply to the question of whether he was in charge of the deal for the buy up of the African countries' foreign debts. Could it still be unknown whether Michael Brown had seen him in Berlin? If so, which passport could he have used to enter the country? However, clearly, it could have been any other passport. In fact, according to his story, he had been living in Berlin under the name of Vlad Holt, which seemed sufficient for the time being. He'd also asserted that his business had nothing to do with the matter.

They'd asked him why he acted as a witness at this trial, and he'd responded that he had something on his conscience. It was painful to him that people got arrested under the mere suspicion of having something to do with the Russian group which had long since dissolved. And they could see that the man truly felt the guilt. He'd spoken in all sincerity. They'd talked to him for two hours or more. He'd requested some tea and a mini cake, then one more, and then another cake and a third. He'd eaten them as though trying to soothe his bitter guilt with sugar. He'd sort of wanted to stop the meaningless arrests, and seemed ready to tell them absolutely everything they wanted – even more so, as over the past twenty years, that information had ceased to be a secret. He'd requested a break to have a smoke. Smoking had taken him a while; one cigarette after another.

"Have you seen how many cakes Vlad eats when he's nervous? That's what I've seen," Richter added.

Who was the man? He surely had some experience that was impossible to conceal, and he truly felt unthinkable guilt. Even Vlad would not have been able to act as well; he'd probably lost the skills over the last twenty years. What about all these hallucinations?

Richter had, for the first time, seen the man from behind a glass in the conference room, through the dim flecks – a vague picture – and for a split second, he'd thought it was Vlad, and instantly feared the man would make some kind of body movement from in which he would come to recognize Vlad. After a second, the man had moved. It had been someone else, not Vlad. They'd exchanged passing glances through the glasswork. Smith hadn't identified him.

"He must be a real Harvey Smith, fuck him. No one has got any doubts, and no one has made a remark like *No, that can't be him*. I actually had some doubts myself. By the way, he's got the genuine passport of Harvey. Where did he get it from?" Maximilian wondered in utter annoyance.

According to Smith, he had suspected the spymaster of the group of being an informant. Yet, he had no idea for whom in particular he might have worked. He guessed that this information had been probably bought from the same by a functionary or someone he'd earlier seen his spymaster with, a couple of times; however, this information must have headed to the CIA, in all likelihood. The functionary used to either forward the information of his own accord, or this information leaked from his hands. As to the question of what had made him suspect his spymaster, Smith had given a reply that it was a mere suspicion; yet he'd been obliged to report. He'd still lingered and then noticed that Moscow had started crosschecking things in a delicate way such as a sudden request to hand over an envelope containing certain paperwork or something less obvious. The group had clearly been investigated. At that point, he'd realized it was time to save his own life, and he'd reported his suspicions to Moscow to avoid falling under suspicion along with his spymaster.

Then a call from Moscow had followed. He had been called in, along with his spymaster. Everyone could well understand what, exactly, that kind of call to Moscow meant. As a rule, a call of that kind entailed a trial and a term in prison. The spymaster had left, and the man had stolen his company's money and fled to Johannesburg, and then even further away. He'd learned that after his visit to Moscow, the spymaster had come back, however, to stay in New York. Soon after, the Soviet Union had collapsed and the group had been dissolved. He'd learned of his former spymaster having been called again to Moscow, facing espionage charges. Smith himself had come to Berlin. For the last ten years he'd been living in Moscow. No charges had been brought against him; he was dwelling on a modest pension.

As to the question of at what point exactly he had reported to Moscow his suspicion regarding the spymaster being someone's informant, Smith had replied,

"It was a year before the spymaster was called in to Moscow and convicted for espionage for the benefit of the United States."

A silence had fallen upon the room. Not everyone must have understood what it was about. Another question had followed,

"Have the people in Moscow been aware of the spymaster being an informant – probably an informant of the CIA – did they do nothing about it, for a whole year?"

"It can't be so. I guess he had been a double agent for a year," the man had responded.

In Smith's opinion, the spymaster had never communicated directly to anyone from the CIA but had only forwarded information through a middleman. It could have been the functionary; the name of which he'd never known, or someone else. For over a year the spymaster had provided misinformation of such a high quality that he had raised no suspicions with anyone. As the situation had turned out to be too dangerous, the spymaster had been called to Moscow and convicted of espionage, which is why, for many years that followed, there was no suspicion that him had brought any false information. The spymaster had allegedly started doing his term in prison.

But had he really been in prison? What could he have told them at that time? The things they must have relied on for twenty years, by taking them for unvarnished truth, had eventually turned out to be a fraud. How could this have been possible? Richter had no clue. It had never come to the surface in any conversations.

Nick was the only person to know what was happening as the whole thing was an invention of his. It was his idea, an incontestable stunner. It was like an olden bomb set under the Agency many years ago, which exploded all of a sudden.

Nick was the first to meet Ivan. He walked down the corridor in the lawyer's office and noticed him from afar, through a number of glass partition walls; he could see the man peacefully drinking tea with mini-cakes. Nick stopped for a second. He caught himself at the thought that this man was exactly the person he was posing for. This man was an agent.

Nick remembered the pale face of Leman, the freckles on his cheeks and around his nose, his bloodless lips, his inarticulate voice and his anxious gestures... the man was clearly not an agent, and this had been evident to everyone around, not to Nick only. Nick had rushed to the Embassy right away and he'd been in time to see Leman abruptly sign his confession statement and hear him ask for a copy of it. Nick had seen him collapse on his chair, searching for cigarettes in his pocket, and heard him spit an oath when he'd failed to find a lighter.

There'd been also Hoffmann standing beside Nick.

"This man cannot be an agent," Hoffmann had reconfirmed with a nod, as if Nick had asked him this question.

Nick came up closer, and the man slowly turned his head to face his stare. Nick almost clashed with Ernest and heard him say in a low voice over his ear, *Here's our cupcake*.

"Is he a Russian? You've promised to give me a whistle. Why aren't you whistling?" Nick wondered, trying to hide his anxiety.

"No, he must have lived in Moscow but just for a short while. I've been looking at him for three minutes now, and for me he is a fine American. I'm sure that in one hour he'll be speaking to you without any accent."

It did not take long to talk to the man. This Smith was "their cupcake" for just one day.

The same day, five hundred thousand dollars came to the witness account in Deutsche Bank.

Naturally, there followed a trace of that money. Yet, this turned up nothing interesting. Except for the money laundering scent, there was nothing much. The witness lived in Moscow, at least. According to him, a week before the court, he'd bought his life insurance with a foreign insurer registered in Panama. This company was, in fact, a broker that worked on behalf of some European insurers. Some of them seemed solid and respectable, and others not so trustworthy. One of the insurance companies was registered in Estonia and appeared to be a duplicate of another German company with a similar name. The company's list of shareholders contained more Russian names. In fact, the majority of insurance policies were registered through this particular company. To all appearances, the insurance agent carried the cash across the border himself. One of the banks in Czech Republic which used to receive the money was owned by the insurance company's founder. From this bank, the money was transferred to the accounts of several other insurance companies on whose behalf the contract was signed, and the brokerage company earned a commission.

As stated in one of the contract's clauses, the client had the right to terminate the contract within ten days by sending notice to the insurance company and could get his money back in his bank account, or where-ever he chose to indicate. This way, the clients would receive considerable amounts on their bank accounts in London or Switzerland. Thus, five hundred thousand dollars had come into the man's account in Deutsche Bank. The tax audit revealed that the money landed on this account upon termination of the insurance contract. Sure enough, this was impossible to do without a prior agreement with the company. It was the most primitive scheme to carry the money that was not taxable out of Russia. Could this witness have been their last client?

That was not the point. This witness could no longer be a witness. What could they possibly bring against him – accuse him of money laundering? Hardly so. He was a good, decent citizen who had signed a contract with an insurer without knowing that this company registered in Panama made its payments through Baltic countries. This money was genuinely his. He had sold his consulting agency. He used to consult on bank-to-bank loans. He had the certificate of sale and the proof of tax payment. Furthermore, this was about Russian money; there was no trace of its foreign origin.

The man would most likely have a really good lawyer. Would he be released on bail, or not? It was clear to everyone that once he was released, he would never be back again. The man must have told them everything they had expected to hear.

The man disappeared the same day. He was steer clear of the surveillance so easily, as if dissolved into thin air. In a café he ordered a cup of coffee, took off his coat, then put it on the chair back beside him and placed his glasses and cell phone on the table. His coat, glasses and his cell phone stayed there, while Ivan was gone. Hoffmann had a reason. Nick was not ready to face a Russian agent. Even having more of his own folks at his disposal he would not be able to resolve this issue, as they did not know the city well enough, like the Germans did, and the Germans... Hoffmann had made it a point that they had to do without surveillance. Neither he nor Nick had a clear understanding of what kind of people they were dealing with. Hoffmann preferred not to scare off the people Ivan might have come with. And they also had no idea about what kind of business this Holt`s widow owned.

"If I see a bug, I'll pick it into the asshole of the guy who put it in," Hoffmann had added in irritation.

Berlin, Train station

When Richter stopped, after a gulp of coffee, I asked in perplexity,

"All of them must have got what they wanted, didn't they? What's wrong there?"

"Everything is wrong. Can't you see it? The man is too good. He is more like a professional robber who is hired to rob the bank from which all the money has been long since stolen," Maximilian intentionally paused and looked at me to make sure if I was able to understand what he was talking about.

"So what?"

"They normally get killed soon after. This is classic."

"We're fucked up with this classic by now," I said through my teeth with subdued fury.

"Smith has recognized Leman, and one could see it."

Richter was right. This was something to think about. Where could this witness have come from? How could he have identified Vlad in Leman's photo? And, if he truly had, to whom would he tell of Vlad being the real Smith, living in Berlin under the name of Leman? And who would eventually come for Vlad? It was a sight to behold, the way Vlad kept staring into the empty backyard from behind the window. He waited and waited in expectation. He was scared of seeing someone in there. And what was worse, he had no idea about whom he was waiting for.

One would think that Vlad had been pretty useless to everyone for the last twenty years; however, flashbacks of that kind seemed to happen.

"Maximilian, do you have an idea of whom this particular witness might be working for?"

Richter said that it looked like a one-time assignment for this witness; the kind he could perform and then disappear – or otherwise, they might assist him in disappearing for good. But in what way could he have known Vlad earlier? And whom could he tell about Vlad? Richter said that he had a picture of that witness, indistinct and pretty useless because the man resembled Vlad like his own reflection in the mirror. The man was considerably older and somewhat more robust, with his features rather coarse, and he was unshaven. However, they would write it off as due to bad climate conditions in Moscow. Richter said that he had already mailed this picture to Victor, and added that he was sure the man had a scar under his chin identical to Vlad's.

Richter told me that he'd felt a nagging pain in his heart once he'd seen that Smith from afar, as if he'd been looking at Vlad's. It was not about their resemblance – the man had a totally different gait and he had no boyhood in him, of the kind of Vlad had...

"That happens when you come find out a woman has cheated on you," he added, putting aside his cup of coffee in a gesture of annoyance. "I felt like I'm being cheated on. Imagine yourself in my shoes. You see him every day. and suddenly understand he's been cheating all this time. I understand that this bastard is just a high-quality fraud, but he can be easily taken for Vlad. He's got sex appeal and charm, a lot of that damn fucking power. This man, When I saw him for the first time, I feared I might lose him. I'm afraid they may kill him after the trial. Can you believe it? I'm as used to death as if it were breakfast time. What is this? Have I turned out to be over-sentimental? Or is this motherfucker indeed that damn good? Listen, I'm a legal counsel. I'm an iron-core piece of crap, but the jury men are common people. He can do to them anything he wants."

I remembered Vlad's words regarding Holt's dead body: that it would still remain in the freezer and it probably had his teeth, and this corpse would keep haunting him wherever he went and whatever passport he chose to use.

And what was this? A living duplicate. He would not really need neither Vlad's teeth x-rays nor his fingerprints; he was indeed the true Harvey Smith, and this sonofabitch was better than Vlad.

I remembered Vlad saying that we usually fail to see things right off the way they truly are, so many things turn out to be mere illusion. And I could hear my inner voice say, *You should not believe that I'm dead until you see my corpse in the mortuary. Look, I've got a scar under my chin... make sure it's truly me. And don't you believe in anything.*

Where on earth could this witness have come from? Hell, I could not even tell which of them was Vlad. The main thing was, where would he go afterwards, in case he survived?

Again, I noticed with Richter the kind of look as if he intended to say something else, but he was still in contemplation,

"I wanted to see you. For how long have you been with Vlad? A month or so? Haven't you got a feeling he's been cheating on you?"

"No. I would have felt it."

"Listen, that bastard is so damn good that I guess many would have a wish to see him dead. And what if he disappeared? Meanwhile, this wish to see him dead may persist. So, Vlad may find himself dead instead. Vlad should disappear. The game is getting too much dangerous. Who has provided for this witness? Who could have invited that motherfucker? He couldn't have come from nowhere ..."

Richter took a rapid glance at me. I had a feeling that he was able to read my face. He did read it.

"A lot has changed over twenty years. The game rules have changed. I'm off-side already, otherwise I would not have come before the investigating judge with all these talks. Is that clear? I'm so badly exhausted from these days." Richter opened his coat wider and covered me with a flap by hugging me with his arm, "Could you kindly hold my balls in your hand, my dear?"

On my way back home in the wet snow, still with no gloves on, I could feel my palm burning with that kiss of his, and I thought, *I shouldn't have an appointment with Richter ever again; this sonofabitch is doing to me whatever he wants.* I wanted to take my hat off in order to cool my head. After taking the hat off, I mumbled, *I'm such a stupid idiot,* and I quickened my pace. By cooling off, I caught myself with a truly idiotic thought, *Good that it happened in a café and not in a public loo, the kind it was last time... and not in the snow bank... I hate having a fuck in the snow.* Before my eyes there floated a wintertime picture of Ilya's apple garden with his face and hands in the snow, and I realized that I would have given anything for it. *Oh god, I wish I were home!*

CHAPTER EIGHT

THE LIVING BOMB

Upon my return, just like that last time on my way back from an appointment with Richter, I found Vlad at the stairwell. It was hard for him to keep inside the apartment. I picked up his cigarette for a couple of whiffs and quickly told him all that Richter had said.

"Vlad, you should go to the world's end now that you're still alive. Richter has a reason. When a man is too good, there is always a wish to kill him…"

"Do you mean you never get to know who I am, in practice?" Vlad said this with a faint smile.

The whole story seemed to consist of endless ravings, to him. He said that he'd stopped getting a clue about anything, much less his own self. He said that he used to be confident and stand by his words and actions. But what if it was someone else; not him? How could one possibly keep the person under control who was doing, on his behalf, anything he wanted; and of whose whereabouts we had no idea?

"Could you end this game, Vlad? In each and every game, you turn out to be a dead man. I can't stand it anymore. I was completely clueless, as we were sitting here and nothing was happening. Now things are different. You've got to flee. Would you like to live in Siberia? Somewhere in a small sweet country house covered with snow, living on frost-bound potatoes? The Interpol would surely get lost in the deep white snow... Vlad, listen, if Victor was here, he would surely send you to Siberia to have a rest, with a kick in the arse. Get the fuck outta here!"

"If the witness has been provided by the British lady, it actually makes no sense. That's it. And don't you try to continue this conversation. I'll decide on my own what I have to do, and what you've got to do, by the by."

"Where could this witness have gotten your passport from? Where could you have left your old passport in the name of Smith?" I asked him, somewhat cooling under his gaze.

"I guess it may have been left with a lawyer, or may have been since long gathering dust in some Moscow archive, along with some other paperwork — who the hell knows."

"How could he have collected it from the lawyer? Through blackmail?"

"By using the password. The spymaster knew it."

"Could he have told this password to anyone?"

"That's absolutely out of the question."

"That is, could they have taken it from the archives?"

"How would I know how they carry out the paperwork from Moscow's archives? It may have turned into a public institution by now. Ask me an easier question," Vlad brushed me off. "Hmm, Richter is afraid the witness may have recognized me and could actually tell someone about it, if only he hasn't yet done so..."

"Yes, should we rather move to a different place?"

"No-no, that does not make good sense. I guess the witness rather fears that I may recognize him. As to his true identity, no one here really knows it, except for the people who've hired him. I may have known him that time, a long time back, but who could it be?"

"What the hell is the difference, if you have to pose for his dead body?!"

Upon Victor's departure, when leaving Vlad and I in this house, he'd told me, meaning it either as a joke or in earnest, *If Vlad has a wish to go anyplace away from here, you'd better break his legs off.* He'd been so damn right there! I thought, *Shit, I've really got a wish to break his legs. How can I possibly keep him safe?!*

Vlad and I stayed till after midnight. We had a considerable number of drinks, and our conversation took a different path.

"Hmm, you've got those freckles, which are hardly visible... So have you been seeking to take over some minor bank all this time?" Vlad wondered, somewhat distracted from his own thoughts.

"Well, with no money, too much regret, that is rather a lottery game, I'm sorry to say so, but there seemed no way."

"And what about that banker of yours?" Vlad started his query.

"I cannot really ask him about it."

"And what about a little kiss on the ass?" he gave me a hint.

"I usually do that: give him a kiss for a good night's sleep; He does not fancy words much, so this is my way of telling him I love him."

"Why are you not with him?" Vlad lit a cigarette, by fixing his icy look on me from above his spectacles. He was looking forward to my reply.

"I do appreciate the way he tells me a thousand lies over a weekend by looking straight into my eyes. I like him being such a bastard, in the full sense of the word. Even when he tells me *Yes,* it really means nothing…" I cut myself short as I noticed that Vlad was, indeed, able to understand me.

"Why is he fond of you?"

"For my being far worse than him. I'm such a bad idealist. I don't know how to explain this to you…"

Ilya had no family. He had not mentioned it a single time in our conversations, and he had never recollected any woman with whom he might have had a family. I could see that the way I was, with my itch for money and my wild ambitions, I was the person he wanted. And then, maybe, he valued something else in me. Sometimes he could see in me a carbon copy of my father, and this ineradicable old-fashionedness of mine rather appealed to him. I must have inherited it from my father, along with that damned idealism of his, of which I found hard to get rid of, as though it were really growing from inside.

Why didn't I have a family? Simply, I was not really interested in men who wanted a family. I was, rather, attracted by men who were about to fuck the world, and who kept running after ghostly millions by living on impossible dreams; the men that were so much like me, whom I used so much while facing them every day, one way or another.

"You're a living bomb," Vlad concluded, chuckling.

"It's fucking true."

Had I have become the way I was while attending lectures at my university? My teacher had hardly had the intention to pass it on to me. There used to be ten of us in the group. And he'd never really taught us anything. Where could I have picked up that kind of ineradicable idealism? Who could have made me a living bomb? He used to tell us that an idea could never come to a blank space; it may only get to be yours just because you find it beautiful. The idea comes to your head when you really put a hell lot of effort to gain it; when you really pay for it. Only then may you see the real face of your idea, as if it were coming out to meet you halfway. It must have been coming from somewhere far away, and the more steps that remained behind, the deeper it was rooted in my soul, and the higher was the price of it, so it was difficult to refuse it, and I could see its face better, little by little. What kind of face held my idea?

It was widely known. Then, why did nobody really find their own idea? It was probably because no one was ready to give his life for what he was doing. And so the idea floated, awash in that sea of life.

One day I picked up a book of Nietzsche, and stayed with it forever. It was a true bomb. And it actually looked like that. It appeared enough to open the book pages so that I'd instantly stood in the shoes of a German soldier frozen in the snows, and I could feel the book warm me from inside. Why was this feeling? Thousands and thousands of soldiers keep opening a volume of Nietzsche, which is their life and soul, the roots of their soul that keep shooting forth in this world the true spirit of the time, so clear and palpable that I seemed able to touch it with my hands. They say that Germans and Russians share a similar kind of metaphysical brainwork. Metaphysics has its own laws that someone had, earlier, named the laws of blood-drenched abstractions.

Indeed, damn it, I could generally feel myself as a soldier lost in the war for money. What about Vlad? True, I could see Nietzsche in him. It was clearly visible in every person that drank in his will for life as if it were vodka. I'd taken so much to life, I seemed to be as undying as a rat, and I could pass on my zest for life like a nasal cold. But what if Vlad and I had acquired two totally different interpretations of the same book?

Wasn't it weird that we both kept eating those Bavarian sausages and felt like Germans? Idealism is free from national background, yet there is a known homeland to it, here, in Germany.

They say that under Stalingrad, two different branches of Hegel's philosophy clashed, and that this Hegel's philosophy could conquer Europe so fast because to the general decline of religion. It was not quite so. The worldview is created by philosophy and not by religion. The philosophical system requires a lot of time, about a hundred years, for it to become a cup of coffee served on the table; for it to integrate into each and every habitual move; into the music in the earphones. No idea grows out of religion. One has to die in order to gain an illusion of life, instead. And I felt disgusted to even touch a dead thing, which was not even in the back of my mind. Thus spoke Zarathustra...

or something like that. I failed to remember it properly. And this sonifabitch was so damn right.

"True, that is why the British Service would always step in..."

Vlad said this in a very low voice. I startled. Could he read my mind? Or was I saying my thoughts out loud? What was this apparition, bloody hell? Had I been drinking too much?

"What? Have I really said it?" I asked.

"No, I'm just a damn good spy, mein herz," he snorted.

"I hope, at least, that you don't really peep into my panties; just into my mind."

"That is in your soul, really. Do you mind making us coffee?"

Indeed, I was about to think of the soul. I felt good here, just because I could see the sky. In these parts the sky was absolutely void, as if there was none at all. I was pulled in by the beauty of this void. Wait. What was it Vlad had just said?

"Vlad, what does the British Service has to do with it, fuck it all?"

Vlad said that it usually stepped in at the point when Germany and Russia started to find common ground. They had never really been able to make an arrangement, despite it being too much easy to achieve. If they had ever managed to do so, Europe would have been under their control. This was against UK interests.

"What the fuck does it mean?" I could not really get it.

"It's amazing how several secret services manage to come to terms within this limited field, the kind of this trial. It's rather like holding negotiations in the loo. And they do come to terms, eventually. They would not be able to agree on any political matters. That means this is free from politics. Most probably, it's all about the money."

Could it be about the money, really? As per Vlad, he did not know, himself, what to think of this court. There was hardly anything bigger than a certain interest in the agents whose files Schumann had bought out. There seemed to be something fishy about it. Why would the banker need those files at all?

"Vlad, could they have been no agents, as such, but some kind of bookkeepers, just like you...?"

"I've been thinking about it all this time. If I could only see that witness, I would be able to tell who he is and where he comes from."

I thought that I would be always able to tell whether a stranger had been a fellow student of mine, if I came across him in the street and exchanged a couple of words with him. One could not get it wrong. It was like a seal; a subtle imprint that remained with us till the last day. My teacher was able to impress his own seal on each and every one of us. We'd come out as books of his. He'd kind of signed each of us with his autograph.

I remembered Vlad telling me that the agents trained at about the same time used to have the same instructors, so they bore something ineradicable and clearly legible from afar. True, it ought to have been so.

I wanted to ask Vlad, *Where have you studied?...* And I almost bit my tongue.

Oh god, it was good that I did not ask this question. Shit, damn it. Was I in time to turn aside? I stared at the coffee maker and absently placed the cups under the hot jet just in time to jerk back my fingers. It only crossed my mind for a second. Hopefully, Vlad could not read the back of my mind. Or could he, really? I hardly had this thought for an instant, and then forgot it right away. It made no sense. Vlad hadn't been to Moscow. And even if he had been there, he'd hardly had a chance to see Kim Philby. Had the man been teaching? Probably so, what else could he do?

Our agents used to be taught by the blown agents that unwillingly preset them for future failure. This was widely known. And still, had it been really so? Who the hell knew.

There was word that Philby had no time for anything; that he had been a ghost of his own self. However, he used to be the British intelligence in the very heart of the Russian Service. Kim Philby is a legend. And legends are everlasting.

As per Vlad, his spymaster used to train him on site by just explaining the needful and nothing else, and Vlad had soon forgotten all about it, as he had never really needed any of this knowledge. He only started to remember certain things now, by fishing them out of his memory like from under stale snow.

I could see the face of my own teacher before my eyes, with that gentle smile of his. I'd heard he was now teaching in Sorbonne. Were they really able to make us what we are, in such an imperceptible way? How could that gentle, intelligent person have made of me the kind of iron piece I currently felt inside? Until now, I believed it must have been due to Ilya.

And could I have been ready to become what he'd made of me? Well, it all must have had a source... Surely. It was supposed to come to you, if you did everything for that purpose.

Taking a rapid glance at Vlad, I thought, *Couldn't this seal get passed from hand to hand as a blessing or a malediction?*

It must have been the same with Jan. He'd seen Holt; however, he had not recognized on him the invisible seal, and he must have realized it was not really Smith standing in front of him, not even an agent.

"Vlad, and what if it was not an event but a particular person?" A guess flashed through my mind.

"Hmm, a living bomb that exploded twenty years after?"

I opened the door, ready to go to bed. Vlad asked me, "What about Richter?"

"No. I can't do it. I can't really hold these balls of his. They're too eely. No-no! Forget it. Let us stop talking about it," I said, and heard him say from behind my back,

"Don't you know a good job is to be done with two hands, mein herz?"

CHAPTER NINE

STRONGER THAN LIFE

Late in the evening when I finally reached the pay phone, I heard Victor's voice saying, *There must be someone else in prison.*

This was already clear. Where could that spymaster of the Russian group be, at this time? Maybe he was collecting coconuts somewhere in the Bahamas or skimming out potatoes at his country house somewhere in the suburbs of Moscow?

What was next?

Curiously enough, this message brought me no relief. True, the banker Schumann was already set free. He would never come back for a trial, but I still could not get rid of the gut feeling that this weird game was far from being over, yet. What could we possibly guess by playing either the Preference card game or mock battles with an opponent who remained invisible? How could one possibly guess his next step?

Vlad had once told me that he was able to guess and foresee the next move. He could not really explain where this feeling came from. He could only sense the handwriting — it was light, as if written in invisible ink on invisible paper. Suddenly, I could see through this handwriting, too. It was light; hardly visible at all. I could feel the pain; the kind Richter had experienced. By listening to Vlad all this time, I must have stopped thinking independently. How could this have happened?

I wanted to get some advice. By stopping in the middle of the street on my way home, I turned on my heels and headed for the hotel, where I dropped in the evenings quite often, as befits the foreigner, then opened my laptop and entered the name of Norman. One day I came across a book of his entitled "The Jackal. Psychology of Terror." Downloading it, I started scrolling the pages. It had to contain the answer on why the intelligence agents were turning into traitors. I already knew one answer: Vlad had told me. But there is always more than one answer. I was not satisfied with the answer I had. I was about to find another one. And I knew it was there.

They became traitors long before they stepped across the threshold with the sign "You will know the truth, and the truth will set you free". And they stepped across it expressly to turn into traitors one fine day. That was the way they saw their career development. They wished to re-act the life of the icon. The legend of Kim Philby made them traitors from the moment they opened that book of his or read about him. This legend kept recruiting people without money or contracts, across time and distance. It recruited everyone near a child's age. The reality appeared helpless against it. It kept dictating its own logic. At this particular moment, someone could be opening the book about Philby, and then in a few years time he would find himself working for the spy directorate in anticipation of an opportunity to launch his own legendary career.

It might come along imperceptibly, once the book of the legend was read through and half-forgotten. It would sprout up deep inside and live to its own time, so that one day it would casually remind of its existence, in an implicit way, and push to make the decision to which one must have been prepared since long ago, with just an occasion being in short supply.

Most paradoxically, such agents appear to be more mature, like everyone who does not really care much about public recognition, awards, money, appreciation and all those matters in connection with a regular, rewarding career. They are do not really fall for the stars and uniform. Surely the traitors get incomparably better money, but this had not been so at all times – yet it would never be the main point. These people rate themselves so high that money does not measure that value. And they are essentially free. No polygraph would be able to determine anything, as such people live in harmony with their own selves and never blame themselves. For this person, there is no border line where they become a traitor; they must have since long slipped across by taking no notice. This implies there would be no trace left on their mind. These people are usually well-educated and highbrow, and as such, are intelligently cruel and deeply calculating.

They are idealists. And that philosophy of theirs makes blood turn to ice. They are like living bombs. This is how the legend of Kim Philby works. And that's a damn good British job.

They say that Philby was disappointed in his illusion and kept unwillingly taking revenge by creating more defectors. He was under suspicion all his life. Be this as it may, people should not be judged by their thoughts; only on their actions. You never know what people could be thinking. I could consider it not a bad idea to have a sleepover with the Roman Pontiff, but as I'm not doing it yet, one cannot blame me for this — it's a mere fantasy.

Philby kept saving human lives, and till his dying day, he probably regretted being unable to rescue the Rosenbergs. There is no denying this, as the man saved not just some abstract lives but millions of people who would never get to know about it. These were concrete flesh and blood people who evaded death, thanks to him. He was a true hero; a legend of all time. The heroes that rescue the world very soon fade from memory. The human heart is not so big and it has space enough for no more than just one love. The world at large is something abstract, and legends suck the living blood, the fresh blood of yet another human who may choose the way of the legend.

The Russian defectors were indeed many, were after the money, and at long last started writing their memories to conceal their greed behind the ideal. There were almost no genuine idealists among these guys.

In fact, an independent thinker can make his own choice as to which side to join, and what to do. There is no law, and no one can tell him what he is supposed to opt for.

Such individuals are dreaded and feared, but this is just a trait of the intelligent people.

After closing my laptop, I thought that every stone in the building constructed by Vlad turned out to be a glass tumbler in a fragile pyramid of glass.

From the hotel, I headed back home as usual, without thinking, took the stairs up, entered, and stopped still by the doors, understanding that I had to leave now, so that I would never see Vlad again. Vlad had been cheating on me all this time. It was betrayal. It could take different form. Indeed, Vlad was a traitor – not the usual kind; but still a traitor.

"What happened? Are you unwell?" Vlad asked as he walked out of the kitchen.

I side-stepped towards the door and sensed with my gut the void of the icy corridor behind my back, the floor covered in the brick rubble, the booming echo, and the sharp air. Realizing that he must have guessed upon seeing my haunted look anyway, I said,

"You aren't Smith."

"But who am I?" Vlad asked me, at a loss.

"I don't know. The ghost that stands behind your back."

"Which ghost?"

"Kim Philby."

Vlad sharply turned away. In the silence that I had never noticed before, I heard a lighter click in his hand. In the black glass's reflection, I could see his face for an instant, lit with his lighter. With a fleeting trace of discontent, he winced as if from snow thrown into his face by the wind. His glance, which I'd gotten used to over these days, seemed alien; there was nothing familiar left. I could now see another person in him, and I would not be able to get rid of that feeling. How could I not have noticed his before? How could I have been so deceived? True, the sonifabitch appeared better than his own self – he was actually better than he seemed to be; he was indeed...

I sprang out into the stairwell. The door briskly closed behind me, by making an unusual squeak against the icy tiled floor. I walked out into the cold. What could I do now? I had to find Victor. I had to... Couldn't I be mistaken? Oh god... I would have never thought that I would lose Vlad in this particular way. I thought, *That is all there is to it. I've lost him*. Along with him, the business was probably lost, too.

And it flashed on my mind, *Shit, among all those pieces of the British crap, Vlad has turned out to be the biggest.*

It would kill Victor. I feared losing Vlad so much, over these days. I unwound my scarf and picked up the pace. A couple of blocks away, I stopped to insert the sim card into my cell phone. I had to make a call to Ilya. He would find a way to warn Victor. Victor could be still in Moscow. Ilya still had a chance to catch him in his flat or office. Maybe…

I could see a message from Ilya on the screen: *The States may request to give him out.*

What was this? This… oh, anything but that. Oh, please, no!

Oh, no, oh god, anything but this. Oh lord, could you please do something! I ran all the way back, hastened by the fear. I felt nauseated. I wanted to pee so badly. *Oh god, I don't give a fuck as to who he may be, just don't you give him away, oh please! He couldn't have left and gone anywhere yet? No? Oh my god, I'll be damned…*

At the house porch, I could see just my own footprints, hardly powdered with snow. After running up the stairs, I pushed the door open,

"Vlad!"

"Are you back already, my dear?"

"Vlad! They may request Smith to be given out to the States!"

"This is mere talk. They currently don't give away anyone." Vlad said this with uncertainty.

"Vlad, we've got to do something! We've got to find your spymaster. Why should it be you? You actually know nothing. You used to have a spymaster. Let him act for you. He is supposed to do so; this is his job. Let them get someone in your place..."

"Mein herz, he's already played a witness for me. Haven't you got it?"

Like this book?

Maybe you leave a review?

ONLY ONE REALITY ONLY ONE REALITY THAT KILLS

Book Four of The Sleeper Series

by Anna Schlegel

ISBN: 9780999127605
ASIN: B072KJ7PTJ

It happens to everyone without exception. It will inevitably happen to you unless you live under the wing of the legend.

He was back. No one believed it was him until he started killing those who had no more doubts.

You may have a wish to learn a bit more on the legendary agent, and these books would most probably catch your eyes. Would you be able to find in them the answer to the question, whether Philby was indeed a legendary spy? I doubt it.

A Spy Among Friends: Kim Philby and the Great Betrayal

by Ben Macintyre, John le Carré

To my mind, it's a better idea to read Phillip Knightley. He starts his book from the point when he stepped across the threshold of Kim Philby's apartment in Moscow. This book has an answer.

Philby: KGB Mastermind

by Phillip Knightley

I'm writing about Kim Philby from a different side, that is from the side where he used to be loved, and where he remains as a living legend.

From Russia with love,

Anna Schlegel

MONEY CAN'T LIE

Book One of The Sleeper Series

by Anna Schlegel

ISBN: 9780998185347
ASIN: B01M1BZR1X

Should there be three pieces of crap this is of the British intelligence classic.

He was not worth a straw to Intelligence; he was a mere sleeper, just a small coin. One day he felt that behind his back there was someone else; someone a big shot of such high value that they could not afford to lose him. Who could that be, - a recent defector? He had no idea.

He could only sense a trace of him, barely-there, just a nip. They were seeking to ward off the trail, and not just by drawing it aside. Now it appeared to lead straight to him. Every little thing pointed to him.

The trace would be lifeless, classically beautiful and as such stone-dead.

WHO SPREADS FOR WHOM

Book Two of The Sleeper Series

by Anna Schlegel

ISBN: 9780998185385
ASIN: B06WLGZ444

The British Intelligence cannot compromise its integrity; it will adhere to its principles like in the old times of rock 'n roll. And it's damn good to see it working... but then, it's scary to see it work against you.

They seemed to be looking for a perfect witness for that legal action. One was a sleeper, another a dead sleeper, and the third was a dummy agent. While this man alone passed for all three, he was never summoned to court.

LIE MAKES ME LIVE

Book Five of The Sleeper Series

by Anna Schlegel

Coming soon

This game of the intelligence, we were either to see through it, or die.

There is an old brain teaser about three different gods, God of Lie, God of Truth and God of Chance. One of them lied all the time, another told everyone the truth only, and the third one could either tell the truth or lie. So who of them was who in there?

Who was that man? There happened to be three people who had told they knew the man. So who of them could be telling the truth? And who must have been lying? Who could have been led up the path? And what kind of person was he himself? He was the only man to know the answer, but he was the God of Lie.

ABOUT THE AUTHOR

Why do I know so much of the Intelligence? It must have come from between the bed sheets, and not just this much. Victor returned to Moscow after a few years of work as a financial expert. He was more of a moneyman than a special service agent, even more he was a swindler. He became a raider like so many others, during those years. He used to have both good luck and failure in bank seizures, in which he lost money. I imperceptibly turned to be just the same like him.

These books are written from an adventurer's perspective. There are no good guys, since those good guys have no chance of attracting a female. Women want bastards.

Why read my books? I've got the undeniable strength of being a Russian author, which means that I'm writing about the Russian Intelligence without using much fiction.

Of course, these are just mere fiction novels, a kind of multi-twist mind game; yet I'm describing events the way they could have touched me in reality. So these books actually represent my "might-have-been" by seizing the fact that I could have lived a number of alternative lives. Understandably, one life is enough for me: my behind would hardly stand more adventures. I'm writing about things that I find interesting. I've only read a few books of spy fiction - for the most part, they are deadly boring.

I was born in Moscow. I studied at the Moscow State University at the Philosophical facility. I got a PhD in philosophy and stayed without work and without money. The financial crisis began. Some years I looked for a work, but took it easy. I became a securities trader in an investment company by chance. And then came the default in 1998. I was without work again.

This was my best time. I became the financial middleman for off-market private transactions. I had nothing. I had been looking for too-big deals. But then there was a time when it was quite possible for me to be the middleman in the sale of a Libyan oil tanker or for the sale of an aircraft abroad. I got sick of conducting multi-million dollar transactions and lost all sense of reality.

I met Victor. Capturing the bank was in my sights. The insider of the bank was its vice-president. I write about his capture almost verbatim. Before leaving, he gave me his three passports... So I do not know his real name. There were no closed doors for him. He had friends from the federal agency for government communication and information from the board of directors of Deutsche Bank. All kinds of people.

Years passed. Victor is long gone. And there are fewer middlemen.

I feel myself to be on the way out. My whole generation is on the way out as well; those who are described as robbing the country.

I like those who robbed the country, and I'm pleased about how it was done. They were really talented financiers; nothing worse than the financiers on Wall Street. They left the country and took the money with them.

Since then, Moscow's air did not smell of millions any longer. But, it seemed to me, it was still in the depths of my house between a pile of white shirts. Now there are no more financial middlemen. The young have gotten jobs first. They receive a salary at the end of the month, and seem to have already forgotten the smell of crazy millions.

It's like being drunk. There's a dizziness from it … They did not want to breathe this air. They did not want to poison their lives. They earned their money. They had wives, children, dogs, and cars, which it was necessary to care of… Their heads have overflowed with thoughts of petty cash.

Then the middlemen were old. And I stayed with them. Therefore, the heroes of my novels are in their sixties. To the former friends who stayed in the stock market, I became infected. No, I just died. And I smell of sweet cadaveric decay. It seemed to me that I was among the dead. And it felt really bad for me, as a living being. But I shared their way of thinking. I was the same as they were: ridiculous and old-fashioned, useless clutter, rubbish. Market garbage. My friends were precisely the same as middle-aged gentlemen.

Sometimes I catch a strange look directed towards me, but then forget about it. The metropolis wiped me from their memory. There was no need to be as nice as kind people who talk with clients and colleagues daily. I had a different way of talking. My talking always led to a deal. And if it didn't, I would give the finger and immediately forget the useless person, as if shaking off dust. And that's all.

I have nothing to regret. I had nothing to blame myself for. Dogs wouldn't blame themselves for their dog's life, would they?

I cannot return to the stock market. It has changed. Brokers, buyers, and sellers have been changed. They all grew up a little. They have got each other for 0.1 percent interest, ready to sell their ass to everyone at 0.5 percent, and would sell their own mother at one percent. I could not do that. The market has kicked me out as garbage.

And the old, among whom I used to be, are gone. The reality of small money has burned out people all around me as fire burns wood. Sometimes it seems to me that I have gone mad; that I live in a world turned inside out. Sometimes I would like to be like anyone... to have a rest, eat, dress, buy a car...

But I can't do it. It would be a living death.

It seems to me I would lose days and years and would end up in devastation and poverty. And I would lose the scent of money, and my skills ... so I clung to the sale of oil, diamonds, and bank guarantees, though I'm sure that it was simply thin air and there was nothing behind it. Sometimes I woke up and thought that all was not with me. But I lived and breathed the air of millions. It was my life. In my life, I gained money from thin air. Emptiness is a magnet for me.

Now I have got nothing. I do not care. I like my life. I like to go for millions. It's impossible to stop me. I might have to be put down like a mad dog.

And I still have a sense of money. I can smell the street's air and say that the market has changed. It smells as sharp as the smell of fresh bread from a bakery in the winter.

THE DEAD BANK DIARY SERIES

THE DEAD BANK DIARY
Book One of The Dead Bank Diary Series
ISBN: 9780986174919
ASIN: B00OPAZQMI

FOR THOSE IN THE SHADE
Book Two of The Dead Bank Diary Series
ISBN: 9780986174964
ASIN: B014Q92DE6

THE PRINTS ON THE SNOWS OF YESTERYEAR
Book Three of The Dead Bank Diary Series
ISBN: 9780986174988
ASIN: B017KYY2MA

SOME DAY I'LL HIT A BANK
Book Four of The Dead Bank Diary Series
ISBN: 9780998185323
ASIN: B01LYZ3XQX

THE FROZEN DEBT
Book Five of The Dead Bank Diary Series
ISBN: 9780998185309
ASIN: B01LX1AKZ7

AUTHOR'S NOTE

In these books there are no cops, no killings. There is much about the illegal takeover of banks, and a powerful amount of money. I know how to pump up a bank, and how to bankrupt a bank. I love beautiful gray schemes on the verge of being crimes. My stories are about fraud through the eyes of a swindler. There are no good guys.

I write about the golden-time bankers, from 1998, when neither the police nor the intelligence services, or any crimes haven't prevented the banks from making money.

These novels are not based on a true story, but you will face this reality in every word.

ABOUT THE DEAD BANK DIARY SERIES

These are stories about a man who is not alive anymore. He was a financier, a retired intelligence officer. I had the good luck to arrange a couple of financial frauds. We bumped into each other before the recession, in the flood of shit, together in the dust.

After his death I still had the power of attorney.

Of course, Victor knew I wouldn't be able to work on his contacts. I had tried. Now it's funny to think of it. I am, and always have been, a go-between, a rat. Nobody needs middlemen. They get rid of them; they send them to Hell. But I had a white shirt with a necktie, and copies of million dollar contracts for oil, gas, diamonds, and rare-earth metals: light as air, rolled fax sheets with lots of zeroes. They made me giddy; they made me drunk. And I ran along with them, and easily foisted them onto the middlemen: muddy, middle-aged misters.

When some of the first deals failed, I went into hysterics. I wanted to throw everything in.

Once I had a dream. In my dream, I heard a telephone call,

"Miss Schlegel? We need your signature to extend a contract concluded by Mr..."

I woke up scared; something turned over inside of me. I realized that I was spending my life waiting for such a call. It didn't matter where it caught me.

But there was no going back. Once you've taken a step forward, you realize you can't turn back anymore.

Why did he leave all this to me? I looked over the papers, recalling past years, deals, people, talks: everything from the first meeting to the last minute. And I couldn't find anything for me; because it wasn't for me, actually, but for the old me. So I changed. I became a con.

My life was changed. Sometimes it was as convincing and disgusting as the life of a whore. It was as inaccessible as the man who despises you. It was like vomit or sweat from the body from a heavy hangover's shivers. You wish to run, but there's no place to run to. It's a cold stupor. So it's stupid to look at the smeared corpse on the road, and it's impossible to regain consciousness to look away. This passion nests in the heart, and you don't know what it is.

I have his photo, the last one, taken at Arkhangelskoe hospital. Summer. We're sitting on the edge of a dried-up fountain. He embraces me with one arm, and I'm lost next to him. He is gray-haired and corpulent. He has a mocking look. And behind us there are towering white marble angels.

THE DEAD BANK DIARY

Book One of The Dead Bank Diary Series

by Anna Schlegel

ISBN: 9780986174919
ASIN: B00OPAZQMI

The rats living on the refuse of the bank's backyard stay full at all time.

This is not a robbery. A bank is taken with all its guts: accounts, debts, points of exchange, the staff to the last secretary, the building. This is beautiful and clean fraud.

I was out of work, while all around you could smell millions, even in the air outside. It was an unforgettable smell of public debt, oilfields, gold, bank guarantees, diamonds... I wanted to breathe in the air of easy cash Moscow, to revel and roll in this air. I could feel the smell of money in the wind on my face. This air was used to make up funds overnight, to make a fortune, to go to rack and ruin and then grow rich again. It was blowing freely across the wreckage of the sold-out Soviet empire.

I was asked to help redeem the debts of a bank. The insider man at the bank held the post of Vice President.

A bit of danger and a bit of love.

FOR THOSE IN THE SHADE

Book Two of The Dead Bank Diary Series

by Anna Schlegel

ISBN: 9780986174964
ASIN: B014Q92DE6

———————————————————

You may live your whole life without getting to know who you are, and sometimes this is for the better.

It was a bank robbery, however this time the gunmen came not for the cash but for the bank itself, and all that followed happened faster than a domino knockdown.

The bank was bankrupted professionally.

Bad debts of the Third World countries, Cuba, Zimbabwe, Morocco, and The Congo have been returned on the bank's balance sheet. Once, the bank sold the debts to itself, to an offshore company.

Who did this?

The banker finds out the bank in Amsterdam... and has taken it over completely.

THE PRINTS ON THE SNOWS OF YESTERYEAR

Book Three **of** The Dead Bank Diary Series

by Anna Schlegel

ISBN: 9780986174988
ASIN: B017KYY2MA

The best one to rob the bank is the banker himself.

The bank, facing bankruptcy, fell out of the hands like a snowball rolling downhill to flattening everything under its weight.

Behind every bankruptcy there are people who make it happen. But there are no influential people. Big figures are absent. It seems you stay face to face with the emptiness.

This happens when the Central Bank is playing against you.

SOME DAY I'LL HIT A BANK

Book Four of The Dead Bank Diary Series

by Anna Schlegel

ISBN: 9780998185323
ASIN: B01LYZ3XQX

The bomb lives to its internal time.

My life became lonely and monotonous, almost mechanical in nature, with a mechanism akin to a ticking bomb. It could be ticking for days and weeks, quiet and imperceptible, to blow up everything around at the right time.

This is the way common folks used to live in the past, bakers and shoemakers. They lived their lives until the revolution burst out. It was their time. And then they went out the door of their bakery and shoe shop for good to take the ministry chairs and cut the heads off the aristocracy, by weaving plots and intrigues. I knew I would not miss my time.

It seemed to me I could go on for another ten years, only to one day stumble on a terse line in the newspaper and realize: my time has come.

THE FROZEN DEBT

Book Five of The Dead Bank Diary Series

by Anna Schlegel

ISBN: 9780998185309
ASIN: B01LX1AKZ7

———————————————————————

When totally nude have a look, maybe you still have the shoulder loops.

One morning he stayed bare-ass, there was no money, no name, no wife, and nothing left... just his shoulder loops.

The deal Victor had set up six years ago kept running like clockwork and suddenly came to a halt. The accounts of the company formerly owned by Victor were blocked by the public prosecution. The man who found Victor in Moscow offered to give him everything back, his company and his board membership and... his wife.

Upon his arrival in Berlin Victor realized that all parties wanted a goner.

And Victor was an ideal goner, as he was also a mole.

Anna Schlegel has a degree in philosophy. She was Securities trader before the recession. The last ten years she has been involved in off-market private transactions as a middleman in Moscow.

Anna lives in Novi Sad, Serbia.

CONTACTS INFORMATION

For information about the author, please visit
TheSleeper.club
thedeadbankdiary@gmail.com

For information about the published books, please contact
Schlegel Press Association at
schlegelpressassociation@gmail.com

www.ingramcontent.com/pod-product-compliance
Lightning Source LLC
Chambersburg PA
CBHW070039030726
47506CB00003B/799